EVEN M
IMPOSSIBLE TALES

To Ara,

Believe and achieve!

D. Worsley

Dan Worsley

Text copyright © Dan Worsley 2021
Cover and inside illustrations copyright
© Martin Spore 2021
All rights reserved

Dan Worsley and Martin Spore assert the moral
right to be identified respectively as the author
and illustrator of this work.

This book is entirely a work of fiction.
Names, characters, businesses, places, events and
incidents are all used in a fictitious manner.
Any resemblance to actual persons, living or
dead, or actual events is purely coincidental.

No part of this book may be used or reproduced
in any manner whatsoever without written
permission from the author, except in the case of
brief quotations embodied in critical articles for
review purposes.

ISBN: 979-8739050335

Also by Dan Worsley:

To Seddy, for being a calming presence, a beacon of positivity and a steadfast supporter.

Contents

Guardian Gnome

The little gnome called the overgrown garden on Anderson Street its home. It had lived there for several years. The gnome had perched, fishing rod in hand, next to the empty pond as it waited patiently for the catch that never arrived. Its once-bright paint had faded. Chunks had flaked off in places. Regular beatings from the outdoor elements had taken their toll on the little pottery creation. It looked weather-worn and unloved.

Inside the house, Kevin grabbed a piece of toast and stuffed it into his mouth before guzzling half a cup of tea. He put down the cup and liquid slopped onto the work surface. Rather than cleaning the spillage, he yawned and hurriedly loaded his school backpack. When he had finished, he slung it over his shoulder and dashed out of the house.

The gnome's head turned. It heard the door slam and the front gate clang. It listened carefully. It waited. It watched for movement. Then it spotted Kevin departing. Quick as a flash, the gnome lifted the fishing rod onto its shoulder. It stood and stretched its aching back, before scurrying stealthily through the long grass. Kevin had moved off at speed and that made the little gnome feel anxious. Losing sight of the boy could be disastrous. The gnome had to catch up with him.

* * *

Kevin waited impatiently at the crossing. His shoe drummed at the tarmac and he chuntered under his breath. It was peak rush hour and the main road was more like a motorway. A constant stream of traffic trundled along. Kevin spotted Amira on the other side of the road. His best friend was shaking her head and tapping her watch sarcastically. Eventually the lights turned red. The traffic came to a halt and Kevin scampered across.

"Morning, Kev. Or should I say afternoon?" said Amira. "Thought you weren't coming. Where've you been?"

"Alarm didn't go off," grunted Kevin. The boy dragged his fingers through his bird's nest hair.

Amira dabbed away toast crumbs that were stuck around Kevin's mouth.

The pair picked up the pace and hurried off to school, unaware that they were being tracked. The little gnome had caught up and was monitoring their every move.

The gnome knew it had to remain out of sight; that was a priority. As it lurked in the shadows, the gnome kept a close eye on Kevin. It had been monitoring the boy's movements ever since Kevin's parents had purchased it from the garden centre in town. The gnome knew the boy's route to school like the back of its pottery hand. It had built up a long list of cut-throughs and hidey holes and was willing to use every trick in the book to fulfil its mission objective.

* * *

Kevin and Amira walked across the schoolyard and blended with the crowds of children. The school bell burst into life and the mass of pupils swarmed into the building.

Peering through a hole in the broken fence, the gnome identified Kevin and watched carefully as the boy left the yard. The little gnome smiled and felt a warm glow of satisfaction thanks to another successful mission. It thought back to the training sessions at gnome academy. Tracking, camouflage, tactical surveillance and survival skills had all proved useful. Smiling cheerily, the gnome squeezed its body under a garden gate and tiptoed across the neatly cut grass. Over the years, it had spent time in many different gardens, but this was one of its favourites. The beautifully tended plot was weed-free and the pond was home to shoals of goldfish that flitted around in the crystal-clear water. Out of all the gardens the gnome had used as a temporary stop-off, it rated this the best.

Not all the garden visits had been so enjoyable. The little gnome had ended up in some horrendous situations. As it scuttled along in the early morning sunshine, the gnome thought back to one such experience. It recalled a garden quite close by, which at first glance seemed idyllic. How wrong the gnome had been! To reach the pond, the little gnome had been forced to navigate countless piles of dog poo in the long grass. Mountainous mounds as tall as the gnome. This was always a bad sign. It clearly signalled the presence of a dog. And the gnome had come to realise, the bigger the poo pile, the larger the pooch.

Sometimes the gnome was lucky and it didn't

encounter the dog. Unfortunately, on other occasions the canine resident had been free to roam the garden. One beastly hound had started to sniff suspiciously at the gnome's head. The little gnome had tried to scare off the pesky pooch by waggling his fishing rod and shouting some naughty gnome words. Sadly, the scare tactics didn't work. Rather than warn off the dog, it seemed to encourage the pooch. Without warning, the inquisitive mutt had raised its leg and proceeded to spray the poor gnome with a shower of warm wee. It was a terrible moment! Reflecting on that awful situation still made the gnome shudder.

Fortunately, things were different in today's garden. No dogs. No dog-poo dodging. And no chance of an unexpected dog-wee drenching. As the gnome settled down next to the pond and lifted the rod from its shoulder, it smiled broadly. It cast out its line then stood as still as a statue. Not a muscle moving. That's how the gnome remained until the end-of-day bell rang.

* * *

The clanging school bell brought the gnome back to life. Yawning loudly, it returned to the hole in the fence and awaited Kevin's reappearance. After a few minutes, it spotted Amira cutting across the yard and running out of the gates. No sign of Kevin. This rarely happened; the pair generally stuck together like glue. The gnome felt its heart quicken and its breathing grew ragged. Do not panic was the first thing they were taught at the gnome academy, but that was proving difficult. Kevin was never late. In fact, the gnome had often imagined the boy half out of his seat and raring to leave at the end of the school day. Most days, he would emerge through the exit doors like a human tornado. But not today. Scanning the crowds of children that were spilling out of the gates, the gnome squirmed uncomfortably.

Over the years, the gnome had monitored Kevin's movements both on his way to school and on the journey home. The school holidays and weekends were the gnome's downtime and it made the most of those breaks. The gnome's legs were often tired after long school terms, so a rest was gratefully accepted. Occasionally, the gnome would spend time with its friend who lived two doors down, reminiscing about the wild nights they had spent partying in their youth.

Anxiety levels rocketing, the little gnome scanned the yard as the flow of children slowed. Despite the tactics picked up during training, panic gripped the gnome like frozen fingers around its pottery heart. Had Kevin slipped the net in the throng of children? How would the gnome elders react if anything happened to the boy? There would have to be some sort of punishment. As the little gnome's thoughts whizzed out of control, Kevin strolled out of the exit doors, seemingly without a care in the world. The gnome breathed a huge sigh of relief and smiled. Panic over, or so it thought.

Kevin removed his backpack from his shoulder and delved inside. He pulled out his earphones. The gnome watched as the boy fitted them and flicked his finger across the screen of his phone. The gnome's smile evaporated. It frowned and tutted quietly. Earphones would make the task more of a challenge. It thought back to a few close calls in the past when Kevin had been lost in his music and the boy's focus had been elsewhere.

Lugging his backpack over his shoulder, Kevin walked out of the school gates. He set off for home with the tunes pumping into his ears. The gnome scurried after him.

Determined to stay close to Kevin, but keen not to blow its cover, the gnome cut through two gardens. It weaved between plant pots and tiptoed across gravel, cursing the crunching under its faded red boots. The little gnome snatched every opportunity to check on Kevin. It peeked through a wire-mesh fence and spotted the boy as he turned onto King Street, which was part of Kevin's regular route home. The gnome, puffing and panting, clambered up a rockery and over an adjacent fence. It scampered across a freshly cut bowling green, taking care to watch out for any humans. Cutting through some woodland, it climbed onto a wall and looked left. Kevin was strolling along, head bobbing rhythmically to the music. He was walking in the gnome's direction.

The gnome ducked under the leafy branches that draped over the wall and peeked out as Kevin strolled past. It smiled a self-satisfied grin. Everything was on track. The boy was safe and the mission objective would be completed for another day. One more road to cross and Kevin would be home again.

Staring intently, the gnome saw the boy stop at the traffic lights at the end of Anderson Street. Kevin pushed the crossing button and waited. The music still pumped into his ears. The traffic lights turned red. Kevin began to cross.

Still perched on the garden wall, camouflaged by the tree branches, the gnome watched closely. It spotted a blue car hurtling along the road, bearing down on the crossing at speed. The gnome sensed imminent danger. It had to act. The time had arrived to put the emergency plan into action. The pottery figure emerged from its hiding place and raised the fishing rod above its head. The blue car, with music blaring from the open windows, showed no sign of stopping. Kevin, who was completely unaware of the impending danger, was now halfway across the road, his head lolling in time with the music.

The gnome zoned out all possible distractions and focused on Kevin. The boy was all that mattered. This was the moment the little pottery creation had been waiting for all its life. Viciously whipping the rod forward, the gnome aimed the fishing hook at the boy. There was no margin for error. It was a life-or-death situation. The fishing line stripped off the reel as the silver hook arced through the air. The gnome temporarily held its breath as the hook latched on to Kevin's backpack. The boy's little guardian reeled at lightning speed, its paint-flaking hands a blur of movement. The fishing line became taut but the gnome continued to reel at high speed as Kevin staggered backwards. The boy's face was a puzzled mask as he tottered and flailed his arms wildly. His movements made him look like an out-of-control puppet being jerked around on its strings.

Straining and grimacing with the almighty effort, the gnome lifted the rod and hauled in its prize catch. Like a felled tree, Kevin tumbled onto the pavement and let out a painful grunt. Sprawled on the floor in a crumpled, groaning heap, Kevin watched as the blue car tore through the red light and barrelled down the road.

The gnome jiggled the hook loose and reeled in the remainder of the line. It watched Kevin as he sat up, looking dazed and confused. A car had pulled onto the kerb and the motorist had dashed over to check on the boy. The woman crouched next to Kevin and wrapped an arm around his shoulders. Kevin waved his hands around and pointed as he explained what had happened. The baffled look on his face reassured the gnome its actions would remain a secret.

After a while, Kevin gingerly regained his feet. The little gnome watched as the boy crossed the road, along with the woman who had gone to his aid.

Suddenly, a wave of panic washed over the gnome. It had to make it home first. The mission couldn't fail at the final hurdle. Quick as lightning, the gnome dropped from the wall and scampered back to the house via a shortcut along the back alley.

It scurried at speed and bounded through the long grass in the garden before taking up its position next to the pond. The gnome snatched a quick glance through the kitchen window. It saw Kevin's mum, her mouth gaping widely, as her son recounted his remarkable story.

* * *

As the gnome basked in the warm glow of heroic pride, it cast its mind back to when it had been created in the aptly named 'Guardian Gnome' pottery. At the time, the factory had seemed colossal to the little gnome and the heat that belted out from the kilns had been unbearable. Production lines of workers decorated the gnomes, using a special paint which contained a top-secret, magical ingredient. The gnome fondly remembered the painting process and the way the paintbrush often tickled, especially under the armpits. It recalled the time it had spent with the other gnomes at the human-protection academy, next door to the pottery. During that time, the little gnomes had been taught the crucial skills they would need to keep their owners safe.

Millions of gnomes have been sent out from the pottery to garden centres across the country. Some of them spent months, even years, waiting to find their forever home. Many people view gnomes as old fashioned or quirky. But those lucky customers who purchased one got much more than a garden ornament. Without realising, they received a minder for life. A pottery protector dedicated to guarding their owner at all costs. So, if you're one of the lucky ones to own a garden gnome, treat it to a fresh coat of paint each year and give it somewhere scenic to spend its days. Take good care of your little gnome – and in return, it'll do everything possible to take good care of you.

I Want...

Olive Upington was a demanding child. If she wanted something, she made sure she got it. Toys, sweets, all manner of treats. Nothing was out of reach for her wealthy, yet weary, parents. They simply caved in to her never-ending stream of requests. Ultimately though, Olive's endless demands proved her downfall, as one day she was taught a lesson she would never forget.

* * *

"Slow down. I can't keep up, love," gasped Mrs Upington, as Olive sprinted along the bustling high street.

Olive stopped dead in her tracks and whirled round to confront her mother. The child's face was scrunched into a scowling rage-filled mask. She looked like a tiger ready to pounce on its prey. "You need to walk faster," Olive snapped, jabbing an accusing finger in her mother's direction. "You move like an old woman. Just look at you. Gasping for breath. Completely unfit. You need to go to the gym."

Olive's mother, struggling to move at speed due to the weight of the bulging shopping bags she was carrying, tried to gently dismiss her daughter's cruel words. "Oh, that's not nice, my little poppet," she replied, and forced an embarrassed smile as an elderly couple stopped to take in the public fallout.

Olive's face was a dark, brooding thundercloud. She seethed with volcanic anger. Her shoulders were raised. Her hackles were up. The anger-fuelled child savoured the opportunity to kick-off another argument which, ultimately, she knew she would win. "You're never nice to me. Ever! If you really loved me, you'd buy me more stuff. That's how it works," sneered Olive, her voice growing louder with every word.

Mrs Upington shuffled closer to her daughter. "My darling baby, please don't say that. You know how much I love you. I just don't want you to step into the road and get run over."

Olive clenched her fists and stamped her foot hard on the pavement. "I'm not a baby! I'm ten years old. I don't need you treating me like a little kid. You've upset me. Big time!" She thumped her fists against the sides of her thighs.

"Please calm down, sweetie pie. I'm so sorry. Let me treat you. Now. Anything. Just name it and it's yours," gushed Mrs Upington, rummaging in her handbag for her purse.

In the blink of an eye, Olive's rage vanished. Her body visibly relaxed. A radiant smile swept across her face. The child reached out and threw her arms around her mother, squeezing her tightly. "I accept your apology, Mummy dearest," she said, glancing through the window of a fancy-dress shop.

The front window of the shop looked like it hadn't been cleaned for decades. It was filthy. The sign above the window was weather-beaten and neglected. The writing was barely legible.

"I want something from that shop. For my Halloween outfit," said Olive, pulling away from her mother and jabbing her finger at the shop window.

Mrs Upington turned around. "Really?! We can get you something from the retail outlet or we can go online shopping. You don't want something from there. The place looks a bit grotty."

Olive narrowed her eyes and fixed her mother with a withering look. The child bunched her fists tightly, causing her knuckles to turn white. "I want something from this shop," she snapped.

"OK. No problem," said Mrs Upington, trying to calm her daughter's rocketing anger. "Let's go in and take a look."

Like a shot, Olive dashed for the door, causing a man on a mobility scooter to weave into the road. "Stupid old fool," the girl called over her shoulder, waving her fist in the air.

Olive barged open the door and hurtled inside, like a human whirlwind. Her mother scampered along in her wake, frowning and shaking her head.

The shop's interior looked tired and shabby. Long strips of wallpaper had peeled off. Dusty cobwebs clung to the ceiling. Racks and rails filled with fancy-dress outfits lined the walls. Masks and all manner of dressing-up accessories were stacked haphazardly on the shelves and crammed into a large glass-fronted cabinet. The items on display in the window were sun-bleached and dusty and looked as though they had been there for years.

A lady was standing behind the counter. She

smiled sweetly at the Upingtons, her eyes twinkling with genuine delight and happiness. "Good morning, my dears," she said enthusiastically. "How are you today?"

As she waited for a response, the lady gingerly leaned against the counter with one hand and massaged her aching back with the other.

"Cut the chit-chat, old woman. We don't have time for it," snapped Olive. "I want an accessory to go with my witch's dress for Halloween."

"OK," replied the shop owner, trying to mask her shock at the girl's lack of manners. "I think I have something that will be perfect for you."

The old lady shuffled slowly towards the display cabinet, her weary bones creaking and groaning with every step.

Olive tutted loudly. "Is she going to take all day?" she hissed. "She's slower than a tortoise with two broken legs!"

Mrs Upington was mortified. A bloom of red appeared on her neck and spread rapidly across her face. She nudged her daughter and raised a finger to her lips.

Olive scowled back a defiant, wordless reply.

"Here we are," said the shop owner, hobbling back to the Upingtons. "What about a witch's hat?"

Olive reached out and snatched the hat from the lady's grasp. She put it on her head and looked in a mirror that was hanging on the wall at a jaunty angle. "Perfect. We'll take it. My mother will pay you," grinned Olive.

Mrs Upington rummaged in her purse. "How much do I owe you?"

"Oh, I don't want a single penny," replied the shop owner. "It brings joy to my old heart that I can make your little girl happy. And hopefully her mum too."

Mrs Upington, slightly confused, thanked the lady for the unexpected act of kindness. Olive, on the other hand, had already walked out of the shop without as much as a backward glance. "Please ignore my daughter. She's lovely, really. Just at a funny age. You know what it's like."

The lady forced a smile and nodded. "Take care and do call again," she replied.

Once the Upingtons had left, the lady sat on a wooden chair next to the till. She shook her head and frowned as she thought about the girl's obnoxious behaviour. Then she thought about the witch's hat. Instantly, the old lady's frown transformed into a grin and she chuckled softly to herself.

* * *

"Ten minutes until dinner. Is that OK, sweetie?" Mrs Upington called from the kitchen.

Rather than replying, Olive sidestepped her way around the piles of toys that littered her bedroom floor. She stopped at the full-length mirror and placed the witch's hat on her head. Although it was a little crumpled and creased, she was pleased with the hat. It looked authentic and would go perfectly with the expensive black dress that was hanging in her wardrobe.

Olive straddled an imaginary broomstick and charged around her room. She raised her finger and twirled it in the air, casting pretend spells on the teddy bears that were lying on her bed. As she came to a stop, she reached up to remove the hat and just happened to glance in the mirror. She caught sight of her reflection and yelped sharply. To her absolute horror, a huge wart had appeared on her chin. It was enormous! It looked like an angry volcano about to erupt. Olive began to prod at the lump, which was the size of a marble. She rubbed it, desperate to get rid of the unsightly growth. Without warning, the wart started to pulse and throb, then rapidly doubled in size. Her eyes bulged and she squealed.

Swinging open her bedroom door, she bolted downstairs like a runaway train, the hat still perched on her head.

Olive burst into the kitchen. "Mother! Mother!" she wailed hysterically. "Look at this horrendous thing on my face. It came from nowhere and it keeps getting bigger. It looks horrific."

Mrs Upington frowned. "Let me get my glasses so I can take a proper look," she said.

Putting on her glasses, she inspected the wart and gasped. Before her eyes, a trio of black wiry hairs sprouted. She had never seen anything like it. The speed of growth was staggering. Mrs Upington gently prodded the hairy lump and frowned.

"Put some cream on it, Mother. Now!" wailed Olive, as tears streaked down her cheeks.

"Probably best to leave it," replied Mrs Upington. "I think it'll be gone by the morning. Dry your eyes then come and get some food. We'll have an early bedtime. It's been a busy day."

Olive harrumphed. The wart drama, combined with the mammoth shopping trip, had taken it out of her, even though she wouldn't readily admit it. Once dinner was over, she reluctantly went up to bed. Sleep arrived quickly and before long she was snoozing soundly.

Unfortunately, Olive slept fitfully that night. Her dreams were filled with cackling witches, bubbling cauldrons, chanted spells and mysterious black cats. The child tossed and turned repeatedly. Each time she woke, she tried hard not to touch the woeful wart, which protruded like a pulsing beacon. Little did Olive realise that when she got up the next morning the wart on her chin would be the least of her worries.

"Wakey, wakey," called Mrs Upington.

She waited until she'd heard Olive stir before she walked back to the kitchen. As she made Olive's packed lunch, she could hear her daughter's footsteps on the creaking floorboards. The beleaguered woman silently prayed that her daughter's wart had disappeared and breakfast would pass off without event. Living with Olive was often like walking on eggshells; one wrong move and World War Three would begin!

As Mrs Upington carried the milk jug to the table, she turned to see Olive stroll in. The startled woman stopped in her tracks. Her jaw hung open. She searched for words but couldn't find any. Her arms weakened and she lost her grip on the glass jug. It slipped from her hand and hit the tiled floor. The jug exploded. Milk and glass sprayed across the kitchen.

The stunned woman raised a shaking hand and pointed at her daughter.

"What's wrong with you, Mother?" asked Olive, staring at the dumbstruck woman.

Coughing out her words, Mrs Upington spoke. "W-w-what's happened to your face?"

Olive fired her mother a perplexed look. "Are you talking about the thing on my chin? Has it got bigger?"

"No," said her mother, shaking her head. "Your face has changed colour. It's…green."

Olive laughed nervously and shook her head in disbelief. Then she dashed into the hallway. Seconds later, she unleashed an ear-piercing shriek.

Mrs Upington navigated her way through the kitchen carnage. When she reached her distressed daughter, Olive was clawing at the green flesh on her face. Her eyes were wide with shock and disbelief. Rivers of hot tears streaked down her emerald-green cheeks.

"What's happening to me, Mummy? Am I ill?" wailed Olive, reaching out and clutching her mother's cardigan.

Without answering, Mrs Upington squeezed her daughter's hands and offered a forced, reassuring smile. The woman's thoughts raced as she searched for a solution to the horrifying transformation that was taking place before her eyes. Out of nowhere she had a lightbulb moment.

The woman raced upstairs and grabbed the witch's hat, holding it at arm's length like it was a venomous snake. She quickly returned to her stricken daughter and draped a towel over the girl's head. Muffled cries and sniffles emerged from beneath the towel.

Finally, Mrs Upington bundled her daughter out of the front door and into the car. "Stay calm, baby girl. We'll sort this out right away."

* * *

The Upington's car lurched into a vacant parking bay outside the fancy-dress shop and came to a halt. Mrs Upington spotted the 'Open' sign hanging in the window. She heaved a huge sigh of relief as she clambered out of the car and tore open the rear passenger door. Olive peeled back the towel. The vision that met Mrs Upington's eyes made her stomach lurch. The shocked woman staggered back, clutching the open door to steady herself. Olive's nose had doubled in size in the time it had taken to drive to the shop. Clusters of angry-looking spots had broken out across her emerald-green cheeks.

Mrs Upington gently draped the towel back over her daughter's face. "Everything'll be fine, sweetie," said her mother, as Olive wept uncontrollably, causing the towel to jerk back and forth. "Come on, love, let's get this sorted."

Olive stumbled out of the car and across the pavement, guided by her mother. The pair entered the shop. Initially, the place was deserted. But on hearing the door bang shut, the elderly lady hobbled into view from the storeroom at the rear of the shop.

Mrs Upington was shaking with a combination of fear and anger. "You need to tell me what's happening to my daughter. Right now!" she snapped, jabbing her finger at the lady.

"Good morning..." she started, but her words trailed off as Mrs Upington whipped off the towel to reveal Olive in her horrific glory.

The girl was now barely recognisable. Her skin was as green as a lizard's scales. Deep crow's feet had developed around her eyes, along with wrinkles and frown lines across her forehead. The hooked nose, complete with protruding nasal hairs, was littered with clusters of small, angry-looking boils. Olive opened her mouth to speak, but rather than producing words she unleashed a burst of high-pitch cackling.

"It's got something to do with this," yelled Mrs Upington, waving the hat around in the air. "I don't know how it's happened, but my precious baby girl has turned into..."

"A witch," added the lady, calmly. She gave a little chuckle. "She's not the first, my dear, and I'm fairly sure she won't be the last. I must say though, the transformation this time has been startling. Possibly one of the most impressive yet."

Mrs Upington fired the shop owner a stunned look. "What?!" she yelled. "You knew this was going to happen?"

"Oh yes," replied the lady, as she began to casually wipe dust from one of the shelves. "Luckily for your daughter, the effects are reversible."

"You're evil! Completely twisted!" wailed Mrs Upington, her arm draped over her still-sobbing daughter's shoulder. "You knew what would happen and you still gave her this cursed hat?"

"Everything's done for a reason, my dear. I can only hope and pray she's learned her lesson," said the lady in a soft voice. "Yesterday, her attitude was nothing short of disgraceful. I saw her. I watched how she behaved outside my shop. It was appalling!"

Mrs Upington was lost for words. Olive tried to speak. More witchy cackles burst from her mouth.

A cascade of tears zigzagged around the spots and boils that had developed on her cheeks.

"It's really quite simple, my dear. One word will reverse the whole process. I think we all know what she needs to say to make things right," explained the lady, flicking away a dangling cobweb with her duster.

All eyes were on Olive. A hushed air of anticipation filled the shop as the two women watched and waited.

"Sorry," croaked Olive in a scratchy voice, her apology followed by another raucous burst of high-pitched cackling.

Within seconds, the reversal began. The green tinge on Olive's face instantly faded, to be replaced by a pale skin tone. The crooked, wart-covered nose reduced in size, and the forest of nasal hairs disappeared. The warts and blemishes were gone in seconds, too. In no time at all, Olive had returned to normal.

The girl looked at her mother. Tears welled in Olive's eyes and regret was etched on her face. "I'm so sorry, Mummy. I treated you awfully. I'll never do it again. I promise," she gushed, throwing her arms around her mother.

Once Mrs Upington had wriggled free from her daughter's grip, she handed the witch's hat to the lady. Without another word, the Upingtons hurried out, never again to set foot in the shop.

The lady looked at the hat and grinned. Mission accomplished! It had proved to be another roaring success. She returned the hat to the display cabinet.

As she turned to walk back to the counter, she heard a raucous commotion outside the shop. The air was filled with the unmistakeable strains of a child throwing a terrible temper tantrum. The lady glanced through the dirty windowpane. She could see a young boy fizzing with rage. The child's father seemed unable to calm the boy. The shop owner winced as she listened to the kid's rants. As the yelling subsided, the shop door crashed open. The child, his face reddened and still screwed up, stomped through the doorway, followed closely by his flustered-looking father.

"Hello, my dears," said the woman, smiling broadly. "Lovely to see you. Are you looking for anything in particular?"

The child grunted an inaudible response. His father shrugged.

"Well, I've got something I think you'll really like," said the lady, picking up a werewolf mask, complete with long straggly hair, fierce orange eyes and sharp, blood-coated fangs. "What do you think?"

Old Dragon

Has anyone ever laughed at you for something you believed in? It's a horrible feeling, isn't it? You're left feeling stupid and like the only person in the world who thinks that way. It's even worse if you're passionate about the subject they're poking fun at.

Well, I've been there and it was awful. Or at least it was until something quite incredible happened that changed my life for ever.

* * *

From a young age, I've been obsessed with dragons. I guess you weren't expecting that. I can see the baffled expression on your face. You're shaking your head in a confused way. Well just stick with the story and keep listening.

I've read every dragon book I could lay my hands

on and researched the subject endlessly on the internet. I filled notebooks with dragon stories and drew pictures that I plastered across my bedroom walls. I even created a dragon blog online, explaining my theory that the mythical creatures still live among us, hidden away from prying human eyes.

As a result, I developed a reputation in the village where I lived. Dragon Girl. That's what they called me. Nobody ever called me Sarah. I liked it at first, I thought it sounded cool and quirky. Then the novelty wore off and I realised people were having a pop at the fact that I loved dragons. That's not a nice feeling, trust me. From that point onwards, I did my best to keep my dragon thoughts and beliefs to myself.

School was particularly challenging most days. The kids showed no mercy and very often had a field day making fun of me. One morning, Candice Bailey picked me out in front of all the other kids on the playground. "Hey, Dragon Girl," she called, as I walked through the school gates, my head bowed. Even though I didn't react, as Dad had instilled in me, she didn't let up. She just called a little louder. "Dragon Girl," she shouted again in a sing-song voice. "Spotted any dragons on your way to school?" Her friends galloped around me. They flapped their arms and mock roared. It was horrible. I felt like every kid on the playground was laughing at me. I hated every second.

Things like that happened quite regularly, but even though school could be tough, the school library was my safe place. It's where I sought refuge between lessons. It was my sanctuary and Mrs Gradon, the school librarian, was my bookish guardian angel. She had worked at the school for many years and was a well-known force of nature. Mrs Gradon wouldn't stand for any messing. In fact, she was occasionally prone to a fiery verbal warning if any kids ignored her library rules. Over time, this earned her the nickname 'Old Dragon', even though none of the kids were ever bold enough to say it to her face!

Despite Mrs Gradon appearing a little scary at times, I thought she was wonderful. I seemed to always find myself on her best side. We got on like a house on fire from the moment our paths crossed. She was always overjoyed to see me, and her smile grew wide each time I visited the library.

Mrs Gradon was a smartly dressed lady. A pair of circular spectacles perched on the end of her nose and a beaded chain of pearls looped around her neck. A tightly pulled bun of grey hair sat on top of her head. It bobbled around like a rabbit's tail as she went about her business. Looking back, I can safely say that Mrs Gradon was one of the few people who didn't have to stifle a grin when I explained my dragon theories. In fact, she stoked my interest and it was largely down to her that my dragon passion had grown. She would dig out informative books so I could get my dragon fix and tell me wonderful stories she had made up. Oh, her tales were incredible! They boggled my brain. The weird thing about the stories she shared was how realistic they sounded. It was almost as if Mrs Gradon had lived the stories she was telling.

"Morning, Sarah," said Mrs Gradon, holding up a book. "Look what I've got for you."

"Mythical Beasts! Oh wow!" I said excitedly, dancing from foot to foot. "I thought it was out of print."

"Librarians can do incredible things, Sarah. Some would say we've got special powers," chuckled Mrs Gradon. She winked at me, highlighting her piercing emerald-green eyes. They were dazzlingly beautiful.

I thanked Mrs Gradon and went to class with the book tucked safely under my arm. The remainder of that day passed uneventfully. If I'm honest, it was probably down to the fact that I was so caught up in my new book that I didn't notice any comments that came my way.

* * *

The following morning, I was dressed and out of the house early. The plan was to fit in my run before school. I pounded along a deserted dirt track and left the village behind as I jogged up through the woods. Shafts of early morning sunlight warmed me as they squeezed through the tightly packed trees. The music from my headphones pumped into my ears and ideas for my next dragon story drifted through my head. I was in a good place.

Gradually, the track grew steeper as it snaked through the woods. To my right was the disused quarry. It looked like a huge bite had been taken out of the landscape. A steep-sided, gaping hole scarred the earth. The workers and their excavating equipment had long since left and, apart from a dog walker or jogger, the area was usually unfrequented so early in the day. It meant that I could be alone with my thoughts and that was just how I liked it.

I glanced into the wooded area, hoping to spot a scuttling squirrel or a wary deer. As I investigated the trees, I stumbled over a rock which sent me staggering. I hit the ground hard. My momentum caused me to roll sideways. The world spun. Gravel grated my bare knees and elbows. It gouged and scored my palms. I rolled off the path and crashed through the bushes at the side of the track, blindly grabbing the foliage to halt my never-ending tumble.

The drop to the quarry floor appeared fast. I screamed in terror as my legs rolled over the edge of the cliff. Frantically, I scrabbled around and clutched hold of a protruding tree root. I gripped it tightly and my knuckles turned white. My legs kicked out into a gaping void of nothingness. My heart thundered in my ears as an icy wave of dread surged through me. Without warning, my fingers slipped. My nails bent back as they raked across the root. Desperate to save myself, I clawed at the soil, leaving long, deep furrows. But it was no use. My body slithered over the cliff edge and I plummeted towards the quarry floor.

As I flailed my arms and legs, it happened. The magical moment that would make my life complete. It began with a single roaring blast that bounced around the quarry walls. Soaring upwards was a dragon. A real-life beast of a thing. It wasn't gigantic like the mythical monsters I'd read about in my books. It had a smouldering nose and a spiked tail. Red glistening scales, like polished rubies, covered its body and a long streak ran across the top of its head, like a grey mohawk.

The mighty beast swooped and caught me mid-fall. I straddled the dragon's body and wrapped my arms tightly around its neck. I could feel its smooth scales against my bare arms and legs. The creature's body heat warmed my skin. I tried to take in what was happening as the beast flapped its long wings and gently glided down to the quarry floor.

I rolled off. My legs felt unsteady so I leaned on the dragon for support. All the time, the creature watched me, intently. A steady stream of smoke puffed from its nostrils and was carried away by the early morning breeze. It raked the ground with its dagger-like claws, carving long trenches. I focused on the dragon's gaping mouth, which was filled with needle-sharp teeth, each one longer than one of my fingers.

The initial feeling of disbelief passed. This was the moment I had waited for all my life. It was the chance to get the evidence I needed to back up my theory. Never again would I be the butt of jokes. Nobody would be able to make fun of me or make me feel silly. I quivered as chills of excitement cascaded down my spine. I pulled my smartphone out of my pocket. One photo was all I needed. But the dragon saw my phone. The beast's bulbous, emerald-green eyes glared at me. The message was unspoken but I understood. Without hesitation I slipped the phone back into my pocket. There would be no photograph. No evidence to finally prove the doubters wrong. A photo would only give the locals reason to hunt down the beast. They would try to capture it. Harm it. Kill it. There was no other option – it was going to be my secret and mine alone. For ever.

In the blink of an eye, the beast stretched out its mighty wings and they started to flap. I stepped clear and shielded my eyes as clouds of dust billowed around me. The downdraught caused the bushes on the cliff edge to rustle. The dragon lifted off the ground. It ascended from the quarry and twisted its body before it sailed off, majestically, and disappeared over the treeline.

* * *

My scratches and cuts were patched up by Dad. They were explained away as the result of a 'jogging accident' – not a lie but sketchy enough to protect my winged saviour.

Later that morning, I breezed into school, head held high and a beaming smile plastered across my face. I batted off the comments as they rained down on me, grinning at the Dragon Girl jibes and wing flapping antics.

I wasn't going to change my daily routine, so I headed to the library. Part of me wanted to confide in Mrs Gradon. She would listen. She would understand. She would believe me. But the risk was too great and it wasn't worth taking.

There was nobody in the library apart from Mrs Gradon. I watched for a few seconds as she replaced books at the far end of the library before she saw me. The librarian placed the books on a table and wandered over. Straight away she spotted the plasters on my palms.

"You need to be more careful when you're running, Sarah," she said. Her emerald-green eyes twinkled as she spoke. "The quarry's a dangerous place."

Her words rebounded around my brain. How did she know I'd been running? How did she know about the quarry? I opened my mouth to question her, but she raised a hand to stop me.

She double-checked the library was empty. When she was satisfied it was, she pulled up the sleeve of her cardigan to reveal a wrinkled forearm. Before my eyes, a row of gleaming ruby-red scales appeared from her flesh. I gasped in astonishment. Quick as a flash, the scales receded beneath her skin and she pulled down her sleeve. I looked at her, dumbstruck.

Mrs Gradon snickered quietly. "I'm a blazopoid," she said, quite matter-of-factly. "There aren't many of us left. We're human-dragon hybrids."

I gawped at her. I had a million questions I wanted to ask, but each one was jammed in my gridlocked brain.

"My parents took the secret to their graves. You're the only human who knows the truth. But I've a good feeling that my secret will be safe in your hands," she continued.

A twister of thoughts twirled inside my head. "Thank you for saving me," I managed to whisper.

"No problem," she replied. "Guess it was just the right place at the right time. Dragons have suffered a bad reputation through the ages. But we're not all house-burning beasts that go around devouring flocks of sheep."

Mrs Gradon smiled warmly before she shuffled off to stack the bookshelves.

As I stood alone with only my thoughts to keep me company, everything dropped into place, like the pieces of a completed jigsaw. I would never doubt myself and consider changing to fit in. From that day, I was brave enough to live according to my beliefs and to follow my heart, every step of the way.

In A Flap

The house at the end of Dale Street was in a state of disrepair. It had been like that for a long while. Ron Griffin had died several years earlier. With no children to help out, his beloved partner, Peggy, was left to look after the place single-handedly. The years passed and Peggy grew older. Time wasn't kind to her. Unfortunately, a string of illnesses prevented her from taking good care of the place. With finances dwindling, the house gradually went to rack and ruin. Roof tiles slipped, the garden turned into an overgrown jungle and paint flaked off the weather-beaten walls. The once-pristine property was a mess.

For as long as I can remember, Mrs Griffin had been kind to the kids in our neighbourhood. She doted on each of us like we were her own.

Even though I'm thirteen, and far too old for hair

ruffles, I still stopped off to see Mrs Griffin. She spent hours in her wooden rocking chair on the porch, sitting in the sunshine watching the world go by. When she saw me, she heaved herself out of her chair and hobbled over. The woman's walking stick helped to support her frail body. She chatted endlessly and told me stories from the past. Mrs Griffin's eyes twinkled like diamonds as she shared her memories. If I'm honest, I think she was glad of the company.

As I walked home late one evening, the old lady's reaction couldn't have been more different. I spotted Mrs Griffin, illuminated under the porch light, perched in her chair with a blanket draped over her legs. I waved and shouted, but she didn't respond. This was unusual and I sensed something was wrong. I pushed open the rotting wooden gate and strode up the path towards the porch. Rather than getting up to greet me, she remained anchored to her rocking chair, head bowed. Something wasn't right. As I got closer, I could see she was deep in thought, a piece of paper clutched between her gnarled fingers.

"Everything OK, Mrs G?" I asked.

Silence. Mrs Griffin was lost in her thoughts.

After what seemed like an eternity she finally

replied. "Not really, Melissa". She held up the paper.

I took it from her. It was a letter. The first thing I noticed was how official it looked. A fancy logo adorned the top of the paper. I scanned the text and skipped some of the long words as I had no idea what they meant. By the time I reached the bottom of the page, I understood enough to know why Mrs Griffin wasn't OK.

"This can't be right. There must be some sort of mistake," I said.

"Unfortunately not. Everything's correct," the old lady replied, forlornly. "I'll be moving out in the next couple of days."

"But you shouldn't have to move away. This is your home," I protested.

Mrs Griffin sighed deeply. I'm sure she caught a tear with her finger before it escaped from her eye. "It's been my home for the last fifty years. It seems that the factory round the back has bought the land, including my house. The boss has had his eye on it for years. My house will be bulldozed to make way for more warehouses, apparently."

"That can't be right," I said. "Surely they can't do that?"

"It looks like they've used some sort of loophole to push the deal through. I'll be paid up, but I don't want to leave. This place is full of memories. I've been a bit silly, really. I ignored all the earlier letters. I hoped it would just go away. But it hasn't. And now it's too late."

I was about to reply when something incredible happened. From a gaping hole in the roof, three bats exploded into the evening sky. Like zooming black missiles, they looped the loop and flitted around. The speed of their movements was astonishing. I watched in awe as they zigzagged and picked insects out of the air. Mrs Griffin gazed up and cooed with delight. She pointed a crooked, arthritic finger at the bats' awesome aerobatic antics. We both watched, spellbound, until the bats ended the show and flew off.

"Aren't they beautiful? They take flight every evening and have done for years. I guess they'll be out of a home too," said the old lady. "They've lived up in the loft for as long as I can remember. Never caused me a bit of bother."

I watched as a lonely tear snaked down Mrs Griffin's wrinkled cheek. My heart went out to her, but I felt helpless. I was only a kid. What did kids know about sorting out serious, grown-up stuff like this?

I bent down and hugged Mrs Griffin. There was

nothing to her; she was skin and bones. The old lady wrapped her bony arms around me. She sobbed softly and I'll admit to shedding a tear too.

Once we had broken our embrace, I didn't know what else to say. I left Mrs Griffin dabbing at her tears with a crumpled tissue. I walked home with the injustice of her situation burning like a fire.

* * *

I was up early the next morning. Really early. I felt groggy. A lack of sleep had left me feeling awful. Thoughts of Mrs Griffin leaving all those memories behind to start again somewhere new had caused my sleep to be fitful and broken. There had to be something I could do to help.

After throwing on my clothes and hurriedly gobbling down my breakfast, I left the house. The sunshine streamed down and was the complete opposite to how things felt in my head.

As I approached the Griffin house, I spotted a car parked outside. Three men were standing by the gate, deep in conversation. The taller man was wearing a smart suit and shades. He looked to be in charge and was doing most of the talking. The other men listened and nodded.

I stepped behind a tree and listened intently,

peeking round the side so as not to be spotted.

"It looks like it'll collapse with a strong breeze. Won't even take a wrecking ball," said the tall man in the shades, grinning as the other two laughed.

"Dead right, boss. The place is a dump. It'll be a massive improvement when it's turned into rubble," chipped in one of the other men.

"Agreed," added the third man. "I can imagine the new warehouse standing in its place. It'll be beautiful. You played a stormer with the old girl, boss. She'll be packed up and gone soon enough."

"Yep. I knew I'd get rid of her easily enough. It was never in doubt. The deadline's midnight tomorrow so I'm sure she'll be packing her stuff as we speak. And if not, the bulldozers can tidy up what's left."

Noisy, cruel laughter filled the morning air. I watched as the two men patted their boss, repeatedly on the back. Their cruelty knew no bounds. I bristled with anger. These men were responsible for uprooting poor Mrs Griffin. To add insult to injury, they had the cheek to stand on the street and gloat about their wicked plan. I balled my fists as anger surged through my body.

I stepped out from behind the tree. "Picking on an old lady. Stealing her house. Are you proud of yourselves?" I bellowed. "You're bullies. That's exactly what you are. Plain and simple."

The three men turned around. Their laughter died away.

"Those are strong words, little girl. You want to be careful what you're saying. We aren't bullies, are we boys?" asked the boss man.

"Nah," replied his sidekicks, in unison.

"The deal's been done fair and square. Well sort of," smirked the boss. "Nothing can stop it going through. It's a done deal. Signed and sealed. The land's mine. Pop along and say your goodbyes to old Mrs G. There's a good girl. Maybe if you play your cards right, I can sort out a weekend job for you, sweeping up in the new factory. Or cleaning the toilets. Would you like that?"

I didn't respond. I simply watched as the three men got in their car and drove off. They tooted their horn and waved out of the windows at me.

With tears of frustration pricking my eyes, I walked up the weed-covered path and knocked on the front door. Mrs Griffin eventually answered.

"Melissa. What a lovely surprise! Twice in two days. I'm sorry I took a while. My back's a bit sore today. I'm packing. The house is cluttered with stuff. Boxes and bags everywhere. I've managed to get a removal van for tomorrow evening," explained Mrs Griffin. "I've sorted a place to rent across town until I get somewhere permanent."

"But you shouldn't have to move in the first place," I snapped. "It's not fair."

"Life feels unfair, sometimes," said Mrs Griffin. "But we just have to get on with it. No point moaning and groaning. I guess all we can do is hope and pray for a last-minute miracle."

I had no words. There was nothing I could do or say that would help. I felt utterly useless.

"You can lend a hand, if you like," Mrs Griffin said quietly. "There's plenty to do."

After loading boxes and wrapping up various objects for what felt like hours, we were done.

"Thank you, Melissa. You're a star. I need to say my goodbyes and catch up with a few friends before I leave."

"I'll come and see you off tomorrow, Mrs G. What time are you leaving?"

"The removal company's booked for six, tomorrow evening. It's the best they could do at such short notice. I know it's late, but hopefully we'll get everything shifted before it's pitch-black. Fingers crossed."

My shoulders sagged. "I'm sorry I couldn't do more," I whispered.

* * *

The following evening, I spotted a removal van trundling down the street. I thought about Mrs Griffin's worldly possessions being whisked away and I broke out in goosepimples. The daylight was fading fast as the van drew up outside the Griffin house. Putting on a brave face, I ran downstairs and jogged up the street. By the time I'd reached the house, the removal firm had already made a start.

"Come on," called the woman who looked like she was overseeing the removal team. "It's going to be dark soon. Let's get the stuff loaded as fast as we can."

Just as she had finished speaking, a car lurched onto the kerb on the opposite side of the street. The three men I'd had a run in with the previous day climbed out and crossed the road.

"Clearing out nice and early. Very much appreciated," sneered the tall boss man. "Knew I could rely on Mrs Griffin's good nature."

His sidekicks didn't attempt to hide their sniggers as Mrs Griffin watched on, broken and weary, from the porch. The fight had been knocked out of her. Within a couple of days, she'd been reduced to a shell of the woman she had once been.

Then something miraculous happened. The answer to Mrs Griffin's hopes and prayers flew to her assistance. The dusk sky darkened considerably. The air was filled with high-pitched squeals and noisy clicks. Furiously flapping wings propelled Mrs Griffin's tiny saviours as they zigzagged and zoomed. The air was alive with bats. What unfolded during the following minutes will stay with me for the rest of my life!

Scooting and swooshing. Flapping and flitting. The bats descended on the three men, like a squadron of dive-bombing planes. Desperately flailing their arms, the men blindly battled the bats. The creatures were a whirlwind of fury and the men tried to fight an airborne enemy that was just too fast and evasive to vanquish. Twirling and whirling, the bats' needle-sharp claws scratched and raked at the men's skin and clothing. The creatures were an invisible foe, swooping at their enemies from all angles.

The small knot of residents who had gathered to see off Mrs Griffin stood and watched, along with the bemused removal team. Jaws gaped. Fingers pointed. Eyes bulged. A cloak of disbelief had been hurled over the onlookers.

One of the men staggered towards the car,

reaching out and pawing blindly for the door handle. Instantly, a pair of bats launched a frenzied attack, forcing him to drag his jacket over his head. The bats corralled the man onto a garden, where he staggered towards a large pond. Splash! He plunged headfirst into the filthy, weed-clogged water. Frogs hopped clear as he splashed around helplessly, a tangled mess of flailing limbs.

Sensing the impending threat, one of the other men made a break for it. He half-ran half-stumbled towards a large waste bin at the side of the road. He grabbed the plastic lid and levered it open. The fetid smell of rancid food wafted from the bin and invaded his nostrils and throat, causing him to retch loudly. Out of nowhere, a squadron of bats veered towards him. They twisted and twirled in a perfectly coordinated attack. The man panicked and clambered into the stinking bin. The heavy lid banged shut and a stomach-churning tide of trash devoured him. Unmentionable horrors entered his mouth as he sank deeper and deeper.

The bats turned their attention to their next target. It was time for the big finale. The petrified boss sought a place of refuge. The cloud of bats descended on the panicked man. Clawing. Shrieking. Flapping. They hung from his clothes and formed a living coat of writhing bodies and beating wings. The tiny creatures flapped faster and faster. The terrified man tried to run for his life. But rather than moving forward he was lifted off the ground. His screams and pleas for mercy were drowned out by the cacophony of noise coming from the tiny creatures. The bats lifted the man higher. He was now hovering above the trees and roofs. They spun him round in a whirling vortex and even performed a loop-the-loop routine to finish off. It was incredible! Then, in one swift movement, they released their captive. The man plummeted towards the ground at speed. He flapped his arms and wailed before he landed, bottom-first, into an overgrown, thorny bush in Mrs Griffin's garden. The needle-like thorns pierced his clothing and buried themselves deep in his skin. He howled and wailed. His ear-piercing shrieks filled the evening air.

As quickly as the bats had appeared, they were gone. They swooped and swooshed through the air and funnelled back through the hole in the roof. The show was over.

All at once, the stunned silence was broken. A woman, who had been walking her dog on the opposite side of the road, had paused to take in the scene. She approached Mrs Griffin, who was in her rocking chair trying to process the mind-boggling batty mayhem.

The dog walker scanned the house. "Do those bats roost here permanently?" she asked.

"Well they do at the moment," replied Mrs Griffin. "But I guess they'll be looking for somewhere else to live."

"Yes, they will," snarled the boss man, who had emerged from the thorn bush looking like a human-hedgehog hybrid. "Stick those little menaces in the removal van and take them with you. You've had your bit of fun now, old lady. Get on your way." He winced as he pulled a long thorn from his bottom.

The dog-walking woman covered her mouth to stifle a laugh. She delved in her coat pocket and pulled out a lanyard with a badge attached, which she dangled in front of the man's face. "I don't think anyone is going anywhere," she said with an assured air of confidence.

The man stared at the badge. His cockiness and arrogance vanished, like air seeping from a punctured tyre. He read the text aloud, slowly. "Pippa Strell. Department for Endangered Creatures." The man's shoulders sagged.

Pippa smiled broadly. "I'm a wildlife protection

officer. I work hard to protect endangered creatures. I'm not sure whether you're aware, sir, or even if you care, but the bats in this house are a protected species. Only a small number remain and this is one of the largest colonies I've ever seen. Destruction of their habitat would be against the law," she said.

The man cursed under his breath. He hobbled back to his car where his two sidekicks were already waiting. One man was wafting away buzzing flies which fizzed around him. The other was drenched to the skin and shivering, strands of pond weed covering his head like a green wig.

As the car roared up the street, the crowd burst into a spontaneous round of applause.

* * *

During the weeks that followed, the local community pulled together to help Mrs Griffin. People gave their time to smarten up her house and garden. Before long, the place was restored to its former glory. Even the bats chipped in by teaming up to fly some of the materials around and lift them into place, although they only helped during the hours of darkness.

Mrs Griffin's future had been secured for as long

as the colony roosted in her house. Lucky for her, bats tend to have a lengthy lifespan, so it was safe to say she would live out the rest of her days on Dale Street.

It sounds a little corny, but I guess you could say they all lived flappily ever after.

Dave

I had lost count of the number of times I'd asked Dad for a pony. Each plea was met with the same response.

"We just can't afford to buy one, Fiona," he'd say. "Do you think I'm made of money? Do you know how much they cost?"

Dad's feelings were crystal clear. The chances of me getting a pony seemed remote. Pretty much non-existent, in fact. After the never-ending stream of knockbacks, I'd written off all hope.

Or at least I had until I arrived home from school one Friday afternoon. I was met by the sight of Dad waving frantically through the lounge window. He was bouncing from foot to foot, his face one gigantic beaming grin. Before I made it to the front door, he had raced to greet me and yanked the door open. He beckoned me inside like an over-excited kid.

"Fiona! Fiona! You're not going to believe what's happened," he babbled, his hands waving around like they were out of control.

Instantly, excitement began to build. I was intrigued and wanted to know more. I needed to find out what was happening. I motioned with my hands and wordlessly urged Dad to spill the news. Judging by the way he was acting, it was going to be something major.

"Eyes closed," he instructed as he walked behind me.

I did as I was told and felt Dad's hands cover my eyes.

"OK, you walk and I'll guide you."

I edged forward. Buzzing excitement escalated with every step. My heart raced; it felt like it was about to explode out of my body.

Finally, we stopped. I could no longer feel soft carpet under my shoes. The floor now felt hard and I guessed we were standing on the kitchen tiles.

"I'm going to count to three and then I want you to open your eyes. Ready?"

I nodded, silently wishing that Dad would just get on with the big reveal.

"Surprise!" shouted Dad, before whipping away

his hands.

Light flooded my vision. It took a few seconds for my eyes to adjust. I blinked away the blurriness. What I saw through the kitchen window took away my breath. Standing in our back garden, tethered to a post, and happily munching the overgrown lawn, was a pony.

"It's a pony!" I wailed, my arms raised jubilantly as I danced around the kitchen. "Oh Dad, you're amazing. Where did you get him from?"

"Well it's a bit of a long story," explained Dad. "A lad at work asked if we could look after him. Just to help out a mate sort of thing."

"Oh Dad, you're the best," I trilled. "Can I go out and see him? What's he called?"

"Dave," replied Dad, with a chuckle. "Funny name for a pony, don't you think? And yes, get out there and meet him."

I didn't need to be told twice. I was out of the house like a shot and scampered over to Dave, who was still gorging on the grass.

"He'll save me hours of mowing time," joked Dad. "He's got a right appetite."

I didn't reply. I was completely in awe of Dave and couldn't tear my eyes away from him. I slowly reached out and patted his back; his chestnut coat was coarse and bristly. Dave lifted his head and I ran my fingers through his bushy mane. It was thick and my hand disappeared deep inside the mass of hair.

"What's this?" I asked, rubbing Dave's head with my fingers. "He's got a weird lump on top of his head."

Dad stepped closer and gently felt the pony's head. He fired me a quizzical look. "I'm not sure, love. Maybe he's banged his head. Or he might have been born with it. Whatever it is, I guess it makes him unique."

I nodded in agreement as I looked Dave over. His mane was knotted and tangled in places and his coat looked in need of some tender loving care. "I think he needs grooming," I said.

"Well that won't be a problem," smiled Dad, as he handed me a plastic bag bulging with equipment. "I'll leave you to it, Fi. I need to sort dinner. I'm sure you and Dave will be best of friends before you know it."

Pulling a stiff brush from the bag, I got to work straight away. Dave shuddered with delight as the brush worked through his bristly coat. He shook his head and wiggled his ears. He was in horsey heaven! Before long, large clumps of hair filled the brush. It looked as though Dave hadn't been groomed for years. But the more I brushed, the more I noticed something strange about Dave's chestnut coat. The strands of hair seemed to shine and shimmer in the late-afternoon sun. The pony looked elegant. In fact, I'd go as far as to say he looked magical.

Next, I moved on to Dave's mane. Using a metal comb, I worked the multitude of knots and tangles out of his long, flowing locks. The more I brushed, the more the lump on his head became visible. I stopped to take a closer look at what appeared to be a bony mound poking from the top of Dave's skull. I gently rubbed it, taking care not to hurt the pony. Dave continued to munch the grass, completely unfazed by my prodding.

I started to join up the dots and a strange thought entered my head. One so unbelievably ridiculous that I guffawed to myself for even considering it a possibility. Rather than being a pony, could Dave be something else? Something quite different?

I moved my head closer to the pony's ear. "There's something special about you," I whispered.

Dave turned his head. He looked me in the eye and I froze in astonishment. The pony's eyes twinkled, like polished diamonds. Then Dave winked at me and broke into a broad smile, revealing a set of huge, stained teeth. The pony threw back his head and whinnied loudly.

This was crazy! Absolutely bonkers! Dave understood what I was saying. He could communicate. I shook my head in bewilderment as Dave trotted over to a fresh patch of grass, leaving my head filled with a whirlpool of swirling thoughts.

Out of nowhere, I heard Dad's voice.

"Wow!" Dad exclaimed as he wandered into the garden. "Great job, Fi. You've made him look a million dollars. Are you ready for another surprise?"

I watched as Dad pulled out a piece of paper from his trouser pocket. He handed it over. I unfolded it and read it carefully.

"You've entered me for a horse show? I've only had a few lessons. I've not even ridden Dave yet. What if I fall off and look stupid in front of everyone? What if he doesn't do what I tell him? The others will all know what they're doing."

Dad smiled and placed his arm around my shoulders. "Stop worrying, Fi. It's not for a couple of weeks so you've got time to practise. Whatever happens, you'll both just do your best. It'll be great and you can show off Dave in all his glory. He's only here short term so make some memories while you're together."

Dad's final comment hit me like a sledgehammer.

I felt the joy and excitement, that had built so quickly, begin to evaporate. The reality of the situation sank in. Dad picked up on it straight away, probably because of my glum expression.

"Don't focus on the fact he's only visiting us, Fi. Look at the great opportunity you've got to spend time with him. Live for the moment."

I forced a smile and nodded as Dad's wise words sank in. There was no point ruining what could turn out to be the opportunity of a lifetime, the one thing I had always wished for. It was up to me to make the most of every second.

After giving Dave a pat on the head, I followed Dad indoors for dinner.

* * *

The following morning, I was up early determined to make the most of the time I had with Dave. As I tore open the curtains, I was greeted by the sight of Dad fitting Dave with a saddle and reins. My heart sang! It was time to ride Dave for the first time.

"Safety precautions," said Dad, as he produced my bicycle crash helmet and a set of knee and elbow pads. "Last thing we need is for you to get injured."

I frowned. "I know money's tight, Dad, but can I get some proper riding gear, please?"

Dad didn't answer but his expression did the talking. He handed over the helmet and pads and I put them on, feeling guilty for making him feel awkward.

"No danger now," I said.

Dad tapped my helmet and smiled before helping me onto Dave's back. "Just get used to moving around the garden first," instructed Dad. "We can try some low-level jumps when you're used to him."

I was excited. Really excited. I took the reins and gently twitched them. "Walk on, Dave," I said confidently.

Dave followed my instructions and began to walk forward, causing me to gently sway from side to side with each lumbering step. Dad watched, smiling from ear to ear, as we completed circuits of the garden, gradually increasing the pace each time until we had built up to a gentle trot.

"I'll leave you to it, Fi," said Dad, "You and Dave are clearly made for each other. You're doing great. I think we'll build some jumps tomorrow if you're up for it."

I nodded vigorously and even had the confidence to take a hand off the reins to wave to Dad as he returned inside. Dad was right. It was like I had a natural bond with Dave; he did everything I asked and was a fast learner. There was a real chance we might just be ready to take part in the horse show without making a total spectacle of ourselves.

After a while, I had lost count of the number of laps we had completed. It felt right to give Dave a break after his good work. I dismounted and looped his reins over the fence. I was about to go to the kitchen for a drink when something very strange happened.

Dave's stomach began to rumble. It gurgled loudly and sounded like water glugging down a drain. I stood next to him and watched. I waited. I knew what was going to happen. And I had a feeling it was going to happen imminently.

Seconds later, Dave's bushy tail began to lift. It looked as though it was being raised by an invisible thread. Then it happened. A moment I'll remember for the rest of my days. Dave trumped! He let rip a thunderous equine explosion that was accompanied by a rainbow puff of sparkling glitter that fluttered to the ground. Initially, I wanted to call Dad so he could witness it too. But I was trapped in a stunned state, watching the trump twinkles vanish into the grass, like melting snowflakes.

Dave hadn't finished. The glitter-infused trump was merely his warm-up act. The starter before the main course. Without warning, a huge dollop of horse manure plopped to the ground. But this horse poo wasn't the usual brown, claggy stuff. Dave's poo glowed for a moment, emitting a bright, almost radioactive, light. I shook my head in disbelief as before my eyes the glow quickly faded, leaving a normal-looking brown dollop of horse manure.

"Oh that'll be perfect for the flowers," said Dad as he wandered over with a glass of cordial for me. "Can't beat a bit of muck to help the flowers grow."

I smiled at Dad. Goodness only knew what effect the glowing horse muck would have on Dad's flowers. But there was no way I could tell him. That was simply not an option. He'd think I was going crazy. And he might even send Dave back to his owner. That was a risk I wasn't willing to take.

* * *

During the following days, I spent every free moment in the garden with Dave. After school and at weekends I was outside with him. The weather didn't stop us; come rain or shine we were together. Dad built a series of fences using road cones and garden canes, so that we could practise jumping.

After a wobbly start, Dave got used to bounding over the obstacles and cleared them with ease. The successful practice sessions boosted my confidence and helped me to believe that we wouldn't embarrass ourselves when our big moment arrived.

As well as constructing the fences, Dad assisted with the mucking out. It wasn't the nicest job in the world, but Dad didn't seem to mind. He scooped up piles of Dave's manure into a wheelbarrow, depositing the dung on the flowerbeds around the garden.

"Dave's droppings will do wonders for the plants," beamed Dad.

* * *

When the day of the horse show finally arrived, I was a fizzing ball of nervous energy. We parked on the gala field, Dave behind us in a borrowed horsebox and me in the car feeling physically sick with nerves. The field was packed with vehicles, horseboxes and trailers, along with horses and their owners and a steadily growing crowd.

"This was a bad idea, Dad," I said, fidgeting with the zip on my tracksuit top. "I'm not going to be able to compete with these kids."

"Stop panicking, Fi. Go for a walk and get some fresh air," said Dad. "I'll sort out registration then unload Dave and get him settled."

I clambered out of the car and walked off, desperate to clear my head.

Rather than calm my nerves, the walk around the field intensified my inner turmoil. The other kids seemed to be wearing smart designer riding gear. Plus, they all chatted like they knew each other. I felt like the odd one out.

I stopped by a horsebox and listened to a conversation between two children.

"Did you take part in the championships last week, Crispin?" asked the girl.

The boy grinned broadly. "Yep. I bagged first place. Zeus is on top form. He's unbeatable," said Crispin, patting the pony standing next to him. "I'm confident it'll be a repeat performance today."

Zeus and Dave were like chalk and cheese. Dave fell into the short, dumpy and loveable category, whereas Zeus was a mighty, muscular athlete with a plaited tail and braided mane. There'd be no way Dave would be able to compete with the likes of Zeus.

Quickly, I made my way back to Dad and Dave. Rather than calm me, what I'd seen had further convinced me that we were completely out of our depth. We'd do well to finish last!

But my concerns eased as I gently stroked Dave's

neck. The pony seemed to have the ability to calm my nerves. "We can only do our best," I whispered in Dave's ear. He turned and grinned.

"Right, Fi, let's get Dave saddled up," said Dad. "You've got quite a long wait. You're last on. Least you can watch the other kids and pick up some tips and tactics."

Once Dave was ready for action, I left him with Dad and wandered over to the arena. The course consisted of several fences, most of which looked considerably bigger and more intimidating than the ones we'd cleared in the back garden.

Suddenly, the public-address system crackled to life. "Our first competitor is Crispin Potterbrook, riding his championship-winning pony, Zeus."

Crispin and Zeus entered the arena. Crispin smiled and waved; he appeared to be oozing confidence. His pony looked elegant and sleek. Zeus trotted daintily around the course, clearing the jumps with ease, and completing a flawless round in an impressive time. The crowd clapped and Crispin raised his hand to acknowledge the applause.

As I watched the following competitors complete their rounds, I feared the worst. I couldn't help but have visions of Dave ploughing through the fences or just flatly refusing. In my head, I could hear the crowd laughing at us. My stomach lurched.

"Come on, Fi," called Dad. "You need to get ready. Not long until your big moment."

I jogged over to Dave and Dad, butterflies flapping uncontrollably in my stomach.

* * *

As we entered the arena, I picked up snippets of conversation from the crowd.

"That kid's wearing a tracksuit. And a crash helmet," said one girl, as she pointed at me.

"Are they skateboard pads?" asked a boy. "She's clearly not used to horse-show etiquette."

"Must be a first-timer. This should be entertaining," added the girl, smirking.

I wanted to turn Dave round and bail out, but the entrance gate had been closed. We were past the point of no return. I took one hand off the reins and gently stroked Dave's neck. My heart rate slowed, instantly.

Dave turned his head to make eye contact. I noticed his ears were pricked and he was listening intently to the children's chatter. He flashed me a wink and then pulled back his lips to produce a toothy grin.

"Our final competitor is Fiona Jenkins, riding

Dave," announced the woman on the public-address system, sparking a polite ripple of applause from the crowd.

Before I could think or worry any more, we were in motion. But rather than starting gently, Dave lurched forward, almost throwing me off. I gripped the reins for dear life and pulled my knees tight into his body. The little pony thundered towards the first jump before leaping high into the air. I could hear the crowd gasp as we sailed over effortlessly, the ground appearing miles below.

As Dave hit the floor, he didn't miss a stride and barrelled towards the next jump. The second fence was higher but this didn't worry Dave. He launched himself at the jump and took flight once again, this time clapping his hooves together in mid-air. The little pony was showboating for the crowd. It was unbelievable!

Crashing down onto the grass, we turned sharply. The crowd whizzed past, a fast-moving canvas of faces and colours. The pony hurtled towards the third fence, tossing his head back and allowing his freshly groomed mane to flap in the air. He was loving every second! Up we soared, Dave turning his head mid-jump to pose for the sea of mobile phones in the crowd.

As we neared the end of the course, the spectators began to chant Dave's name. They loved him. They'd taken him to their hearts. The pony's ears were pricked and the sounds funnelled into his head. The crowd's reaction seemed to energise Dave and he responded by galloping even faster.

We headed for the final fence; a mighty creation which even Zeus had found a slight challenge. But Dave wasn't intimidated. He galloped at lightning speed, his clattering hooves a blur of movement, before lifting off the floor and easily clearing the top bar of the fence. As we glided through the air, Dave delivered his big finish. Raising his tail, he unleashed a ferocious blast of wind, followed by a twinkling stream of sparkling dust which created a beautiful rainbow effect.

The crowd's reaction was deafening! Clapping and cheering invaded my ears as we crossed the finish line and came to a stop. I gripped the reins tightly as Dave reared up on his hind legs and performed a celebratory jig.

The spectators had never seen anything like Dave. A wave of people surged into the arena and surrounded us. Hands stroked Dave and patted me on the back. Eventually, Dad battled his way through the throng of spectators and helped me off the pony's back.

"How did you teach him those amazing tricks?" asked Dad over and over, like a stuck record.

I shared a knowing look with Dave. "I guess he saved his best performance for the big day," I replied, gently ruffling his mane.

* * *

Once things had calmed, we were awarded first place; it was a magical moment! Dave wore his winner's rosette with pride. He spent most of the day posing for selfies, flashing his trademark toothy grin in every photograph, including one with a star-struck Crispin. It was a perfect end to what had been an incredible time with Dave.

"We made the most of our time together," I said to Dad once we'd managed to get away from Dave's adoring fans. "I'm gutted that he'll be leaving us, but I'm sure we'll still be able to see each other."

Dad smiled. He had a glint in his eye. "Well, I think you'll see a lot more of him," replied Dad. "He's going to stay with us. Permanently."

It felt like there were fireworks exploding in my heart. I wrapped my arms round Dad's waist and hugged him. Dave threw back his head and let out a loud, victorious whinny.

"There's a special bond between you two. We can't break that," said Dad.

"But how will we afford to look after him?" I asked.

"Don't you worry. I've worked it all out," replied Dad. "Judging by the way my flowers have grown over the last couple of weeks, I reckon we can make an absolute fortune selling Dave's manure. I've already taken loads of orders today. The stuff's amazing! I've never seen such colourful flowers. And they're at least twice the size they normally grow."

I beamed. "We might even end up stinking rich," I chortled. "Literally."

Double Digits

"Do you think today's the day we'll finally go outside, Aunt Annie?" asked Felix, his crossed fingers shoved deep in his pockets.

Aunt Annie forced a smile. "Not today, Felix, but it won't be long now," she replied, trying to sugar-coat the pill. Without another word, she continued to clear the table following their evening meal.

Fobbed off yet again. Felix sighed and shook his head, frustratedly. His shoulders sagged. The boy radiated stone-cold disappointment. He watched Annie move to the sink, the flickering candlelight throwing her silhouette across the room. She began to wash the pots as the boy chewed over his next move.

Scraping the wooden chair across the tiled floor, Felix stood. He walked to the window. The heavy wooden shutters, which were closed day and night, blocked out natural light completely. Felix wished more than anything in the world that he could look through the window, just for a few seconds. He craved a peek at the outside world. Over the years, the artwork that decorated the shutters had begun to fade. Paintings of mountains, forests, lakes and animals he and Annie had created. Views that Felix yearned to see but could only ever dream about. He turned to see the woman busying herself at the sink. Quick as a flash, he reached up and pulled the metal bolt that held the shutter in place.

Annie heard the bolt clunk and turned around. Her face was frozen in horror. "Felix! Come away from the window. Now!"

The terror-stricken woman bounded across to the boy, bridging the gap in a couple of steps. Felix jumped back in surprise. His face was ashen. "Just a quick look, Aunt Annie. That's all. Please."

The woman gripped the boy's arms and caught sight of the black squares on his wrists. The symbols that had confirmed Felix was the special one. She moved him away from the window. Clear of any possible threat or danger. Aunt Annie paused momentarily then ushered him down the narrow corridor. Felix wriggled and writhed like an eel every step of the way. She guided him into his bedroom.

The boy turned to see the woman struggling to get her words out. Little did he know how desperate she was to share the truth. She wanted to cast away the lies. To end the whole act once and for all. But she knew it was not an option, at least for the time being. Without uttering a word, she slammed the door shut and slipped the bolt across.

Felix listened intently as Annie's footsteps faded. Defeated once again, he slumped on his bed and sighed. No TV. No radio. Just a handheld games console to keep him entertained, along with his collection of books. Reading and gaming were his only means of escape. The boy scooped up a dog-eared book off the floor and began to read.

After battling sleep for a while, Felix popped in his earplugs and finally dropped off into a deep slumber. He had grown to like the pin-drop silence the earplugs provided. In fact, he couldn't remember a time that he hadn't worn them.

Meanwhile, Annie sat alone in the lounge, preparing for the inevitable nightly event. She waited. Wished. Wondered. Worried. She wrestled with the guilt that weighed heavy. Lying to Felix went against everything she believed. The level of deceit had grown over the time they had been together.

Ultimately, she understood the mission. Her actions would contribute to the end goal if they made it that far. It was up to her to do everything within her powers to protect the child. To guard him. To put her life on the line. Felix's safety and wellbeing were paramount.

Annie's body jerked as the lights flickered. She felt her heart thump faster as the floor gently trembled. The terrors that haunted the hours of darkness had arrived once again.

* * *

The next morning, Felix stirred early. Half-asleep, he turned to see the door open. Annie peeked through the crack between door and frame. She smiled warmly as Felix removed his earplugs and smiled back with a lop-sided grin.

Annie walked in. The woman's face was emotionless and her body language awkward. She sat on the bed next to Felix, who was still stretched out on his back as he came to terms with the start of another day.

"I'm sorry for last night. But you must listen. How many times have I told you never to touch the shutters? It's for your own good. For our safety."

The boy listened intently but didn't reply. He

stretched out his arms and yawned. Then he sat up next to his aunt. Sensing the unease in the air, Annie placed a hand under his chin and slowly raised his head. Felix struggled to make eye contact.

"Why do we never leave?" blurted Felix. "I'm sick of being caged up. I feel like a prisoner. You must too."

Felix's words hit Annie like a punch in the gut. She composed herself quickly and slipped an arm around his shoulder. Annie drew a deep breath and prepared another half-truth.

"It's hard to explain. All I want to do is keep you safe. That's what I promised when you came to live with me," she said.

"But when can we go outside? We've been here for so long and we haven't been out once. Why?" fired back Felix.

Aunt Annie sighed and bowed her head. The older Felix had grown, the more he kicked back against the rules. As a young boy, he had accepted everything and her role was relatively easy. Now he'd become a challenge. But regardless of his age, the last thing she wanted to do was build up the boy's hopes. "It's complicated. I guess you need to trust me. Just believe me when I tell you that it won't be long."

Felix frowned. Surprise, surprise. She loved to drop in the complicated line.

Suddenly, there was a loud bang on the front door. Annie stood and scurried out of the room, followed closely by Felix. Weaving their way along the narrow corridor and through the lounge, they headed to the front door just in time to hear a second knock. Annie reached out and pulled a short metal lever on the wall. Felix watched as a large hatch opened in the door.

"Delivery day again," said Annie, excitedly. "Let's see what we've got today."

A gun-metal grey box slid through the open hatch in the door. It clanked as it hit the floor. The hatch snapped shut as Annie pushed the lever. The pair picked up the box and lugged it to the kitchen.

Felix watched intently as Annie unloaded the food. He assisted her by putting the cans and boxes in the cupboard. Annie handed toiletries to the boy, who scurried through to the bathroom to store them.

Once he had left the room, Annie grabbed a letter from the box and hastily shoved it into the pocket of her jeans. When the boy returned, she was waiting for him, hands behind her back.

"There's a surprise in this week's delivery, Felix," teased Aunt Annie. "Would you like to see it?"

Felix's face illuminated as she whipped her hands from behind her back to reveal a paperback book and a computer-game cartridge. She waggled them from side to side. The boy lunged forward and in a blizzard of smiles and thanks he grabbed the gifts.

"Let's call them your early birthday treats. Ten tomorrow. You're growing up fast."

Felix wasn't listening. He had already made a start on his new book, reading as he walked back to his bedroom.

As he disappeared out of sight, Annie pulled the letter from her pocket and perched on the stool in the kitchen. Her eyes whizzed over the text and an anxious look stretched across her face. She shoved the letter back in her pocket and sighed deeply.

* * *

The following morning, Felix bounded into the kitchen. Rather than starting his tenth birthday with a smile, Annie sat at the table and stared vacantly into space.

"Everything OK, Aunt Annie? Do I get the day off lessons because it's my birthday?"

Annie snapped from her trance and pulled out a chair. She motioned for the boy to join her.

As Felix sat down, he noticed tears welling in Annie's eyes.

"I'm sorry," blurted Annie. "This isn't how we

should be celebrating your special day."

A knot formed in Felix's stomach. Something felt wrong. Very wrong. He threw Annie a confused look.

The woman drew a deep breath. "I'm going to tell you the truth. No more lies or stories. You need to listen carefully. What I'm about to say might confuse you. It might be hard to understand. You may not even believe me. But before I start, I want to apologise for the times I've been dishonest. It's just the way it had to be."

Felix stared at his aunt. Tangled thoughts and endless possibilities swirled through his mind.

"First things first, Felix, I'm not your aunt. My name's Annie Millbank. Professor Annie Millbank. I'm a government scientist. You've no idea how important you are, Felix. You're a special little boy."

Felix's brain whirred at high speed as he tried to process the woman's words. He wanted to ask questions but equally he needed to hear more. A scientist? The government? Why was he so special?

Annie reached out and gently rolled up the boy's shirt sleeves. The pair looked at the black squares under the skin on Felix's wrists. "These confirmed you were the one we were looking for. These marks are the signs we were seeking. And when we heard your name that just confirmed our hopes. Felix means lucky in Latin. Ever since we discovered you, it's been a case of shielding you from the dangers that lurk in the outside world."

"But you said they were birthmarks," blurted Felix. He scrunched up his face and shook his head as he chased the story threads that were dangling before him.

"Those marks alerted us to your ability. They're a sign of your gift. Your superpower!"

Felix laughed out loud. "Sure thing! Like the superheroes in the movies?" he asked, sarcastically.

Annie didn't reply.

"OK. Let's go along with the story that I'm some sort of superhero. Why wait until today to tell me?" asked Felix.

"Because today you've turned ten. Double digits. According to our research that means double the power. Today, your special ability reaches maximum."

Felix pushed back his chair and stood. He ran his thumb over the black square outline on his left wrist. His brain worked overtime to process the staggering information.

"Cool. So when do I get to use my 'special gift'?" he chuckled.

Annie's face was set like granite. She stared at Felix unblinkingly. "Tonight," she replied.

* * *

A short while later, Annie pulled open the door and welcomed a visitor. He was a well-built man dressed in smart military uniform. He had a green duffel bag slung over his shoulder.

"Is the boy ready to be briefed, Professor Millbank?" asked the man, smiling at Felix.

"I believe he is, Colonel Briggs. I've done my bit so it's over to you," she replied.

The colonel placed the heavy-looking duffel bag on the floor and drew up a chair next to Felix.

"Right, son, you need to listen and listen good. You've been holed up in this military safehouse for long enough. It's time for you to go into the big wide world again. We'll keep you safe, but you need to do your bit. We've prepared well for this. Let's not stuff it up at the final hurdle."

The boy sensed tension in the colonel's voice. Felix made eye contact and gave the man his full attention.

The colonel nodded in the direction of the bag. "Everything you need's in here. There's a special helmet with a night-vision visor. You've also got an all-in-one suit made of steel mesh and high-tech fibres. There's a pair of protective boots too."

"What am I going to do, exactly?" asked Felix.

The colonel leaned back in his chair and stroked his chin. "You're going to be the kid who saves the world."

Felix's eyes grew wide. "What?!" he yelped, completely bewildered.

"I'll give it to you short and sweet. The world's been taken over by a plague of odd socks. It's bad, kid. Really bad. They've formed an odd-sock army and their aim appears to be global domination. They've even mutated. Most can fly. And worst of all, they've developed a taste for human blood! They're nocturnal and only leave their daytime hiding places to run riot during the hours of darkness. The outdoors is a no-go zone at night."

Felix stared at the colonel in stunned disbelief. "What?! Odd socks aren't bloodthirsty beasts. They're just lost pieces of clothing that drop behind the radiator or get stuck in the drum of the washing machine. Or even get swept under our beds."

The colonel stroked his moustache and snickered softly. "Well that's where you're wrong. These odd socks have escaped into the wild and mutated. And there are lots of them. Think of the socks you've lost and then multiply that by everyone on the planet. The last estimate was in the billions. We're overrun with the things and pretty much out of options how to stop them."

Felix waited for the colonel to laugh and jab him lightly in the shoulder to signal the whole thing was a big joke. But the man's face didn't crack. He remained serious and focused. "O-K," said Felix slowly. "What will I do to end this psychotic sock plague?" He tried hard not to smirk.

The colonel narrowed his eyes and his brow furrowed. The man's chair creaked as he leaned closer to the boy. "This is deadly serious, son. Humanity is under threat. Many lives have been lost already. Don't you dare joke around."

Felix gulped and sat bolt upright in his seat.

"According to our scientists, your body now contains enough energy to destroy every one of those socks. The scientists will tell you more when they brief you. But from what I understand, it's going to be like those shooting games on your little computer. You'll point your wrists and blast away!"

Felix shook his head in bewilderment as he eyed the black squares on his wrists.

"Don't stress, kid. It'll all be fine. Go and put on the gear. Then we can get this show on the road," instructed the colonel.

Felix lugged the heavy bag to his room and returned a few minutes later, fully kitted out. "Are you coming with us?" he asked Annie.

The woman frowned and shook her head. "I won't be with you in person, Felix, but I'll be with you in spirit. You can do this. I know you can."

"Come on, son. No time to waste," chipped in the colonel. "You're going to see Professor Millbank again before too long." The colonel forced a smile.

Neither Annie nor Felix smiled back. Instead they wrapped each other up in a gigantic embrace which only ended due to the colonel's forced cough to signal that he was ready.

Felix slipped on the helmet and flicked up the visor. The colonel ushered the boy out of the safehouse. As the door banged shut, Annie slumped into a chair in the lounge. All she could do now was sit tight and pray.

***

After a nerve-shredding wait, the moment finally arrived. The safehouse lights flickered. The floor quaked. Both were signals of the return of the footwear foes. Annie hadn't seen the enemy, but she had heard many terrifying tales. Sickening stories of socks attacking people, hunting down the humans on the streets and much, much worse. It had been the stuff of nightmares.

But then Annie had discovered Felix and the young orphan boy had given the world new hope. He would be the key to bringing the odd socks' reign of terror to an end, once and for all. He would restore night-time normality. And that was why Professor Millbank had shielded him with great care for so long.

When the battle began it was intense! Clouds of socks veiled the night sky. They swarmed and writhed high above Felix's head, an ominous army of escaped footwear. Once the numbers had swelled well into the hundreds of thousands, they came at the boy from all angles in a carefully coordinated attack. Ankle socks, knee-high socks, patterned pink socks, smart-looking work socks and furry loungewear all joined the odd-sock onslaught. They flapped their material wings and zoomed across the jet-black sky. The open end of each sock gaped wide, like hungry mouths ready to feed. The ravenous footwear could smell the little boy. They craved human blood and were ready for a Felix-sized feast.

The young boy fought back his fear and followed the scientists' instructions carefully. Visor pulled down and his night vision activated, Felix picked off swathes of socks, blasting them with the bright-red laser beams that emitted from the squares on his wrists. The boy's reactions were lightning quick, mainly thanks to the countless hours of gaming he had completed during the safehouse lockdown. The attacks were incessant, but Felix retained the upper hand as an endless stream of socks were turned into fiery balls of burning material. The boy cremated the flying footwear, sending the flaming remains flapping to the ground.

The battle was hard-fought and arduous. Felix's energy levels dipped, but he was resilient and drew on every ounce of strength to fulfil his destiny. The young boy battled hard as the socks continued to flock his way, like moths to an irresistible flame. The countless pieces of footwear communicated. They sent out distress calls that brought even more socks hurtling at supersonic speed from around the globe. It was an unrelenting wave of fearsome footwear. However, each sock, whether it was a small, vicious-looking trainer sock or a thick, slow-moving woollen garment, met the same fate. They were all obliterated.

* * *

As dawn arrived, an eerie silence consumed the safehouse. Annie was still slumped in the chair in the lounge. She hadn't slept a wink and tiredness fogged her mind. Just as her eyelids began to slowly close, she jerked awake as the front door creaked open. Standing in the doorway was Felix, his face drained of colour and his outfit filthy. Behind him was the colonel, his hands tucked under the boy's armpits as he gently supported Felix's weakened frame.

"It's over," said the colonel in a hushed voice. "Our little saviour needs to rest and recharge but he was desperate to see you first."

Annie dashed to the boy and cradled him in her arms. Tears of relief and joy flooded her cheeks. The boy's sock-slaying, world-saving exploits had exhausted him, and he allowed Annie to support his limp, weary body.

"We did it, didn't we?" mumbled Felix in little more than a hushed whisper.

"You did it," Annie corrected, more tears welling in her eyes. "I never doubted you for one second. I knew you'd sock it to them and save us all."

Look Into My Eyes

I'd like to think of myself as unlucky rather than badly behaved. My teachers and parents would probably disagree. They'd tell you that I've deserved the countless detentions, groundings and tellings-off that have come my way over the years. Maybe the odd time, if I'm honest, I've had it coming, for sure. But on most occasions, I didn't set out with the intention to cause trouble. It just happened.

One particular incident springs to mind: the time the house got trashed. I genuinely didn't mean for it to happen. Honestly. No word of a lie. You must believe me. Listen carefully and decide for yourself once you've heard the full story.

* * *

I'm a twelve-year-old boy. An average sort of kid. I

wouldn't stand out in a crowd. Unfortunately, for some unknown reason, trouble has found its way to my door on more than one occasion. Yeah, I'm mischievous and I'll hold my hands up to that. Like the time I tried to kidnap, just for laughs, the light-up Santa from Mr Bilson's Christmas display. I ended up blowing the power supply to the whole neighbourhood. That wasn't a shining moment! Or when I managed to cause an evacuation at the swimming baths, leaving everyone shaking and shivering outside on a freezing cold November afternoon. And I won't even start to go into the gory details about the time I got Mum arrested on a day trip to the city.

You see, I'm a bit of a practical joker. Always up for a laugh is how most people would describe me. I'm a sucker for it. A laughter magnet. I wouldn't do stuff that might cause long-term harm or distress. Unfortunately, things just seem to snowball. Little jokes or gags blow up into massive catastrophes. But none of them will ever compare to the time I tried to hypnotise our family dog, Dreamer.

I had always been fascinated with those TV hypnotists. They put members of the audience into a trance and get them to do or say crazy things. I remember seeing one bloke acting like a bird, strutting around the stage pecking at imaginary seed. He kept flapping his arms and sticking out his bottom, pretending to do a birdie walk. The whole thing was hilarious. The audience were in fits of laughter.

That TV moment stayed with me. Witnessing hypnotism on the telly made me wonder if I could do the same with Dreamer, our family dog. Dreamer was a Great Dane and a smashing pet. She was a huge beast of an animal and looked more like a small horse than a dog. She was so distinctive that everyone recognised her as she lumbered around town on her daily walks.

There was one major flaw in my plan. Apart from TV shows, I had no idea how hypnotism worked, so it seemed like a long shot. Possibly an impossibility, I guess you could say. I researched hypnotism online. After hours of clicking through internet websites, I stumbled across one that made hypnotism seem straightforward, almost an idiot's guide. I scoured the information and discovered that all I needed was a watch on a chain. No problem! When Grandad passed away, he'd left his ancient pocket watch to Dad. I just had to find it.

Dad's drawers were filled with all sorts of junk. Stuff that most people would have long since thrown out, but Dad kept 'just in case'. It drove Mum mad. She called him a hoarder.

After much rooting and rummaging, I felt something shiny and smooth in the bottom drawer. As I pulled out the object, the light from the bedroom lamp glinted off Grandad's gold pocket watch. I ran the metal chain between my fingers. It was perfect and virtually identical to the one I'd seen on the website. I pocketed it and ran downstairs.

Mum and Dad were putting on their coats by the front door. "OK, love. We're off into town for some shopping," said Mum. "We won't be long. Can we trust you for half an hour on your own? No silliness."

"Of course," I replied.

"Righty-ho," said Dad. "We'll be back ASAP."

Quick as a flash, I shut the door and whistled for Dreamer. The huge dog bounded towards me and sat obediently in the hallway. I fished the watch out of my pocket and dangled it in front of Dreamer's face. She looked disinterested at first, but as I began to gently swing the pocket watch from side to side the movement caught the dog's attention. Her eyes followed the pendulum-like movements.

"You are feeling sleepy, Dreamer," I said, reading the script on my phone screen. "Very, very sleepy indeed."

Nothing happened. The dog had lost interest in the moving watch and was now scratching herself.

"Oh come on, Dreamer. You need to concentrate on this. Let's try again."

I whistled to grab her attention. Then I started to swing the watch in long arcing movements. I spoke in a low voice and dragged out my words, very slowly. "You're... really... sleepy. You... can't... keep... your... eyes... open. You're... under... my... spell."

Dreamer sat bolt upright. She stared at me with glassy eyes. Her chest barely moved. My heart felt like it had skipped a beat as a rush of excitement flooded my body. I pocketed the watch and waved my hand in front of the dog's face. Nothing! Not even a blink. I clicked my fingers, but Dreamer didn't flinch. It had worked!

"OK, Dreamer, I want you to pretend that you're..."

My thoughts hurtled at breakneck speed. Ideas flooded my fizzing brain. I could make Dreamer do anything. Be anything. The options were unlimited. I could have picked a budgie and Dreamer could have flapped her legs like doggy wings. I could have chosen a kangaroo so the pooch could have hopped on her hind legs. Nope, I was going all in.

"...a dinosaur," I shouted, excitedly.

Instantly, the dog opened her mouth wide, bared her teeth and bark-roared. The noise was weird and like nothing I'd ever heard. I staggered back, blasted off balance by the doggy-dino roar, and fell onto the stairs. Dreamer turned and barrelled down the hallway, crashing from one wall to another, like a bowling ball bouncing off bumpers. The pictures on the walls, which had been perfectly aligned, were now hanging at jaunty angles. One of Mum's favourites had fallen to the floor and the frame was broken and the glass shattered.

Dreamer charged on at speed towards the kitchen door. "Dreamer! Stop!" I yelled.

It was clear the dog wasn't going to listen. I was about to shout again. But before the words could leave my mouth, she ploughed head-first through the door, splintering the wood and leaving a huge dog-shaped hole. Lots of crashing and banging followed.

"No, Dreamer! Stop!" I hollered, as I set off in pursuit of the doggy dinosaur.

When I arrived in the kitchen, I was confronted by a scene of chaos and carnage. Pots and pans littered the room. Mum's best crockery, which she saved for special occasions, was smashed to smithereens and strewn across the laminate floor. Cupboard doors hung open. Tins of food were lying in the contents of a burst-open bag of flour, which coated the floor like freshly fallen snow. Next to the kitchen table, a bag of pasta had split open and the twirls had spewed out across the floor. The canine tornado, however, was nowhere to be seen. She had already moved on.

CRASH! Dreamer was in the lounge. The sickening sound of shattering glass gave that away. It sent my tummy into turmoil. I abandoned the kitchen carnage to follow the dog, scooping up a couple of loose dog biscuits from the floor on my way.

The sight that met my eyes when I entered the lounge made my heart sink. The high-definition, state-of-the art TV, which Dad looked on as his pride and joy, was face down on the carpet. Wires snaked out of the back of the trashed telly. It looked like an explosion in a shoelace factory. Mum's ornaments had been swiped off the mantelpiece and were lying on the carpet. Dreamer had clambered on to the sofa. She was bouncing up and down, raking her claws across the cushions. Stuffing bulged out from the long rips. Dreamer pulled at the white filling with her teeth, ripping out mouthful after mouthful.

Suddenly she spotted me. She looked wild and angry. Out of control. I stood my ground as she watched me intently.

"Does Dreamer want a treat?" I asked, waving one of the bone-shaped biscuits in the air.

Dreamer continued to stare at me. A long rope of drool dribbled from the corner of her mouth. The string dangled on to the cushion and formed a wet mark.

Pouncing off the sofa, Dreamer bounded across the lounge towards me. Springing up, she launched herself into the air. Legs outstretched, she hit me hard in the chest and knocked me flying. I crashed down on my back and Dreamer landed on top of me. The dog was a dead weight. She pinned me to the floor. A long drool string dribbled onto my face and oozed down my cheek. I wriggled my hand free and pushed the treat close to her mouth. Dreamer sniffed at the biscuit. Then she gobbled up the tasty snack, leaving my hand plastered in a thick coating of dog slobber.

The mutt opened her mouth and gave a bellowing dino-dog roar before clambering off. She then shook herself vigorously. Long strands of gloopy dog spit splattered on the walls. One particularly thick string of drool slithered down the mirror over the fireplace. Dreamer then turned tail and hurtled out of the lounge.

As I got to my feet, I could hear the dog thundering upstairs. Pounding paws and clattering claws rattled up the wooden stairs. I tried to unpick the tangled thoughts that were swirling in my head. I needed a strategy to end this canine chaos. And fast! I pulled out my phone and scrolled through the hypnotism website. There it was. The answer to my prayers. The single word that would bring Dreamer out of her trance. All I had to do was make eye contact and say the word.

Tearing upstairs, I followed the noise which led me to Mum and Dad's room. Bedding was spread across the floor and I arrived just in time to spot Dreamer's tail as she scrabbled underneath the bed. Seconds later, the double bed levitated as the dog hoisted it on her back. I watched in sheer disbelief as Dreamer careered across the room and wiped-out Mum's dressing table, before slamming the bed against the wall.

Then there was calm. Silence filled the room as I waited for Dreamer to emerge.

Grrrrrr! An angry protest burst out from beneath the bed.

"Come on. Good girl," I encouraged.

The growling stopped. I lowered myself into a crouching position and ducked my head so I could peek under the bed. Like a flash of lightning, Dreamer made a break for it.

I grabbed her collar and tried to stop the dog in her tracks. But it felt like I was trying to slow down a runaway truck. Dreamer was a big, strong dog. Dino-Dreamer seemed much bigger and a whole lot stronger. As I clung on to her collar for dear life, Dreamer continued her rampage. I hung on tightly as she thundered across the landing. My body slithered along the polished wooden floor as she dragged me by her side. But then Dreamer headed downstairs.

"No!" I screamed at the top of my voice. Unfortunately, she ignored my plea.

I clunked and bumped down every stair, twisting and turning, moaning and groaning, but determined to keep hold of the rampant dog's collar. The stairs bashed my ribs and dug into my legs. The pain was agonising.

As Dreamer reached the hallway, close to the front door, she fleetingly turned and we made eye contact. "Cease!" I yelled.

Instantly, the cloudy look that had filled Dreamer's eyes lifted. Her trance had been broken.

I heaved a huge sigh of relief, just as the front door opened. Mum and Dad stood frozen to the spot in the doorway. I flashed them a smile and waved from my sprawled position on the floor. They didn't respond. Instead, they looked beyond me into the kitchen and the lounge. Mum's eyes bulged. Her mouth gaped open, like a fish gasping for air. She made a strange whimpering noise and the colour drained from her face. Poor Mum lifted her arms and clamped her trembling hands to her colour-drained cheeks.

"Don't get worked up. I can explain what happened," I said, adding a huge dollop of fake confidence.

"Explain?! Explain?!" roared Dad, as frothy spit gathered in the corners of his mouth. "I can't wait to hear what you'll come up with this time."

Dad's face and neck had been swamped by a crimson tide of rage. A pulsing vein throbbed on his forehead. His fingers had transformed into claws, which he was flexing menacingly. He was seething with a volcanic anger and I was sure he'd erupt at any moment. I'd seen him upset on many occasions, but this time one thing was for sure: I'd seriously rattled his cage. Dad raised his claw-hands and his face scrunched up with fury.

Then it happened. Amid all the chaos and turmoil, I had my shining moment of genius. It was a fiendishly clever plan that would lead to the trashed house being tidied and my bacon being saved.

Quick as a flash, I whipped out the watch and started to swing it in wide arcs. Dad's anger melted away instantly as he focused on the watch. Mum's eyes had glazed over and were also fixed on the swinging timepiece. "You're... feeling... sleepy. Very... sleepy... indeed," I said, as a relieved grin swept across my face.

Out Of This World

Something was inside the cardboard box. Whatever it was seemed keen to escape. A scuffling, raking sound told me that. The noise sounded like the captive was trying to scratch its way out.

I dumped my bike on the pavement and edged towards the box. My empty newspaper bag swung by my side, like a pendulum. I watched the box for any movement, half expecting something to leap out and pounce on me. Then it happened. The moment I'd remember for the rest of my days. I watched the cardboard flaps slowly open. A glistening purple hand, made up of a thumb and two fingers, reached out. The limb didn't look like anything I'd ever seen. It wasn't of this world. Without warning, one of the spindly fingers beckoned to me.

Feeling like I was under the spell of a hypnotist, I

edged closer. I leaned forward and peered into the box. The mind-boggling sight bewildered my brain. My eyes flitted between the contents of the box and the deserted street. Icy chills cascaded down my spine as my breathing grew more ragged by the second. Peering at me was an alien being.

It was only small, probably the size of a kitten. The bizarre-looking creature's bulbous, ink-black eyes stared deep into my soul. I watched as it tilted its egg-shaped head to one side. Its chubby, purple body seemed to emit a luminous glow, like a lamp. I watched carefully as its body pulsed and throbbed. I was mesmerised and terrified in equal measures. My out-of-control heart was hammering against my ribcage as my confused mind tried to work out what was happening.

The creature stretched out its arm a little further. One of its fingers glowed brightly as it began to write a message in the air. It looked like sparkler writing, the words temporarily appearing before my eyes. I could make out the message as clear as day: HELP ME.

For a split second I considered grabbing my bike and making off. This was all just too crazy. But the creature clearly needed assistance. Plus, it would have eaten me or blasted me with a laser if it were on some sort of evil mission.

I began to close the cardboard flaps. The creature was pleased. Its pinprick mouth formed into a tiny smile and it even gave me a thumbs-up before it ducked down. This was all getting more bizarre by the second! I scooped up the box and slid it into my empty newspaper bag. I raced home, my legs working like pistons as my newspaper bag and its intergalactic contents swung by my side.

* * *

My plan was simple: keep the creature away from Mum. She'd freaked out when I'd brought tadpoles back from the pond, so I couldn't begin to imagine her reaction to an extra-terrestrial being stashed in the house. She'd flip, for sure.

I propped up my bike in the garage and crept into the house through the back door, the box tucked under my arm. The house was silent. Mum was still in bed, so I tiptoed upstairs like a ninja, avoiding the creaky steps.

As I stepped on the final stair, the creature started to scratch wildly at the box. I stopped dead. I was going to get rumbled! I put my face close to the box and made a quiet shushing noise. Instantly, the scratching stopped. The creature's purple hand pushed open one of the flaps to give me a reassuring thumbs-up.

I tiptoed into my room and sat on the bed. I put the box on my lap and opened the flaps. Two ink-black eyes peered back, unblinkingly.

"You'll be safe with me, little one," I said. "I don't know what to do yet, but I'll get you home. Somehow. You just need to be nice and quiet, so I can keep you a secret."

Another thumbs-up. It knew that I'd look after it. The alien trusted me. But I guessed, realistically, it didn't have many other options.

I tried to think up a plan. My gut feeling was to stash the creature under my bed, but it would be game over if Mum cleaned my room while I was at school. Plus, what would happen if the alien went walkabout and trashed the place? Mum would kill me. There was only one thing for it. The creature was coming to school.

I pushed the box into my backpack and zipped it up, leaving a little gap for air. By the time I'd got changed and grabbed some breakfast, Mum was up and about.

"Morning, love," said Mum, still looking half asleep.

"Hey," I replied, warily eyeing the backpack which

I'd left on the table.

"Good sleep?" asked Mum, filling the kettle.

I opened my mouth to answer but the words were caught up in my throat. The alien's arm was poking out of my backpack. The purple limb wiggled around like a snake being charmed from a basket. I watched as its hand blindly fumbled about before it grabbed an apple from the fruit bowl and began to recoil, slowly.

I watched its every move and willed the creature to move faster.

Mum switched off the tap and began to turn. I had to act. And fast! Like a sprinter bursting out of the blocks, I crossed the kitchen in three huge bounds. I swept up Mum in a gigantic hug and twirled her round.

"Oh, Archie. You're such a sweetie," she giggled, as water sloshed inside the kettle.

I smiled and held Mum close. I manoeuvred her so that her back was to the table. And that's how we stayed until the alien's hand, still clutching the apple, had disappeared back into the backpack.

"Righty-ho, Mum. Got to shoot," I said, finally releasing her from the never-ending embrace. "Catch you later."

I scooped up my bag and grabbed my bike. As I

whizzed along, I chatted over my shoulder to the creature. I must have looked completely bonkers, seemingly speaking to myself. The only response I received was a rip-roaring burp once the alien had devoured the apple. The creature may have been small in stature, but the belch it unleashed was an absolute beast. I was stunned! Suddenly, the apple core whizzed out of my backpack and landed on the pavement, bouncing and spinning, as I raced off to school.

* * *

I hurried into class and sat down for the first lesson of the day. I grimaced and groaned. Monday morning was always a killer start to the week. Double history with Mr Smith. Ugh!

The alien had settled, fortunately, so I stashed my backpack under the table, well out of sight. Just as I sat up, the classroom door flew open and smashed into the wall. The books on the shelf wobbled and teetered. Standing in the doorway was Mr Smith, his face screwed up like a scrunched-up piece of paper. He resembled a human volcano about to erupt; ready to spew anger and rage across the classroom. The children fell quiet. Pin-drop silence. Bottoms were stuck to seats and eyes were glued on the man-mountain of a teacher as he lumbered into the room, an air of menace filling the space.

"Right, you horrible lot," he growled. "Let's see who's got their homework."

I heaved a sigh of relief. I'd completed mine and stashed it in my bag. Then my blood ran cold. The homework and the alien in the same bag. This wasn't going to end well. I listened as Mr Smith worked his way down the register. Finally, he reached my name.

I fumbled in my backpack and pulled out the shredded remains of my homework sheet. It looked like it'd been mauled by a tiger.

"I can explain," I said in barely more than a whisper. "It's been a bit of a topsy-turvy morning."

Mr Smith glared, nearly cutting me in two with his icy stare. I watched as his moustache twitched, like a wiggly caterpillar. He sighed and calmly placed his pen on the desk. He removed his circular glasses and tucked them in his jacket pocket. Then he strode towards me. A twisted grin appeared on his face and he began to wring his hands.

"Oh, has it?" he said. "I suppose that's a good enough excuse for destroying your homework?"

He was close now. He stopped walking and began to tap the toe of his shoe on the floor. The anger was building. It wouldn't be long until he blew his stack.

Mr Smith took a sharp intake of breath. It felt like he was sucking the air out of the room. His legendary, primeval roar was about to be unleashed. I braced myself.

But then something happened. Something that could not have been more badly timed. The alien trumped. Not a little squeaky one. Or a silent, sneaky one. It let rip the biggest, loudest bottom blast I'd ever heard. The smell that followed the windy expulsion was like nothing I had ever experienced. It was not of this world! The nauseating, stomach-churning stench invaded the classroom, drifting around like a poisonous fog. A ripple of giggles whizzed around the room before silence took over again. Some children pulled their jumpers over their faces. Others pinched their noses. Some wafted the whiff like they were battling an invisible enemy. One girl even started to gag uncontrollably before she ran out to the toilet, her hands clamped over her mouth.

"That wasn't me, sir. Honest." I said in little more than a whisper. "I can explain. It was..."

My voice trailed off. Mr Smith was beyond reasoning. He was shaking with anger. The alien trump had been the final straw. As I braced myself for the verbal tongue-lashing of a lifetime, I glanced down and spotted a purple finger poking out of my backpack. The tip was glowing.

A bright blue bolt of light radiated from the creature's fingertip. It momentarily illuminated the classroom with a dazzling light. Everyone shielded their eyes.

As I gently removed my hands from my face, I looked at Mr Smith and let out a gasp. His mouth had disappeared. It had been erased. Deleted. Wiped away. The class stared in stunned silence as the stricken man clawed at his face, his eyes wide with a mixture of horror and bewilderment. At the same time, Mr Smith made a strange, muffled noise as he tried to plead for help.

Before long, the word was out and help arrived in the form of Miss Sheridan and Mr Caton. They walked the mouthless man out of the classroom and away from the gawping gallery of stunned kids.

The children in my class spent the rest of the day providing accounts about the moments leading up to the mysterious disappearance of Mr Smith's mouth. Luckily, no-one had seen where the flash of light had originated. It was at that moment I realised I needed to ditch the alien. It was just too unpredictable. Yes, it had saved me from a telling off, but keeping it was too risky. If the creature could erase a man's mouth with the flick of a finger, what else was it capable of doing?

* * *

Fortunately, the alien kept a low profile until the end of school. I'd thought things through and it was time to get rid of my intergalactic discovery. I decided to take the box and its contents back to the spot where I'd found them. The creature could make its own way home. If it got here, it could get back. I climbed onto my bike and was just about to set off when my path was blocked by Eddie Stump and his band of bullying cronies.

"You're in a rush," grunted Eddie. "You got time to show us what's in your backpack?"

A shiver ran through me. I couldn't hand over the alien to Eddie and his mates. I had an idea what they would do with it and it wouldn't be pretty.

"It's none of your business," I fired back, barely able to disguise the fear in my trembling voice.

Eddie scowled. He began to menacingly pound his fist against the palm of his other hand. "Am I going to have to come and take that backpack off you myself?" he asked.

Before I could answer, he lumbered towards me, his sidekicks fanning out as part of the well-coordinated ambush. They had me surrounded! I scanned the yard. No teachers. No help. No way to escape. Suddenly, I heard the zip on my backpack slowly open. Eddie and his band of bullies stopped in their tracks. They stared in stunned silence as a blinding flash of light zipped from the alien's fingertip. The beam whirled and danced in the air then hurtled towards Eddie.

Instantly, Eddie's belt vanished into thin air and his trousers dropped to his ankles, revealing a red pair of flowery underpants. A look of horror swept across his face as he began to turn crimson. He started to stagger. His arms windmilled as he tried to keep his balance. Within seconds, he was teetering precariously. Like a derelict tower block being demolished, he toppled. The beast of a boy crashed onto the floor, his flowery red undies on show for everyone, like a floral warning beacon.

Not wanting to miss my opportunity, I powered out of the school gates. I pedalled like my life depended on it. As I glanced over my shoulder, my heart plummeted to my trainers. Three of Eddie Stump's sidekicks were in hot pursuit. I had to lose them. I weaved around pedestrians, cutting down back alleyways, trying every trick in the book to shake them off my tail.

I cut across a patch of wasteland at the back of school. The area was deserted. Momentarily, my pursuers were out of sight, but I knew they weren't far behind. The muscles in my legs burned. It was a warm day and sweat had saturated my shirt. I was running on empty. Tears pricked my eyes as I thought about the alien ending up in the cruel hands of Eddie's gang.

Suddenly, the sun disappeared. A swirling wind, whipped up from nowhere, caused me to slam on my brakes and skid to a halt. The sky vanished and a dark shadow swallowed me. It felt as though the biggest cloud in the world had swept across the sun.

I looked up to see a colossal, silver disc-shaped object hovering overhead. Multi-coloured flashing lights blinked and danced, creating rhythmic patterns.

I felt a wriggling movement in my backpack. As I took it off, the zip slowly opened and the alien emerged, its dark eyes staring at me. But rather than pleading for help, its expression had changed. It almost seemed at ease. Relaxed. Relieved. At peace.

From above, a blinding light shone down. The creature, for one final time, gave a thumbs-up. I smiled and nodded. Then it slowly levitated into the air, hovering in the light beam a couple of metres above my head. In the blink of an eye, the alien vaporised and the spaceship disappeared.

Clouds rolled across the blue skies and the sun blazed down once again. It felt as though the spaceship had never been there.

* * *

Within twenty-four hours, news crews had flooded the town. The out-of-this-world incident had gone global. TV stations clamoured for interviews. But I kept my head down and my mouth firmly closed. The secret was mine to keep for eternity.

Eventually, the story became old news and the incident was dismissed as a well-crafted hoax. Theories about shadowy government projects, low-flying aircraft and even some far-fetched idea about a secret weather-controlling device proved extremely popular too. Mystery shrouded the whole event and I was more than happy to leave it that way.

Although my time with the alien now feels like the weirdest, craziest dream in the world, I know the events that day were real. In fact, I have proof – in the form of a glowing blue orb, which I discovered hidden deep in my backpack. I like to think of it as a little 'thank you' gift that shows the creature's appreciation. And what a gift it is! The orb does something mind-blowingly brilliant. But that's a whole different story which I'll save for another day.

Acknowledgements

This book wouldn't exist if it weren't for the supportive, incredible team I've got behind me.

Sarah 'Seddy' Seddon has constantly been a shining beacon of support, especially when the waves of panic and insecurity threatened to wash me away. A calming influence, a neutral opinion and a firm believer in my literary mission, Seddy has backed me all the way. She is a superstar and I'll be forever grateful for everything she's done.

As always, I'm sad that Mum didn't get to read these stories, but when I am struggling and the solution suddenly springs to mind, I'd like to think it's down to Mum's help from afar. Dad has supported me with his listening ear and words of advice, proving to be a reliable sounding board and voice of reason.

When the super-talented Martin Spore agreed to be involved again, I was over the moon. Martin's illustrative wizardry and design skills are mind-blowing and it's a joy and an honour to work with him.

Once again, Kevin Barber has done a super job with the formatting and layout of the book's interior.

Kevin's skills and knowledge have proved invaluable and despite numerous requests for alterations and last-minute tweaks, he never complained.

When the stories are taking shape, fresh eyes and honest feedback are vital. I'd like to thank Barbara Strachan and Lesley Bennett for their involvement during these early stages.

The Tales are written for children, so I need young readers to let me know what they think about the new stories. Ben and Rebecca Essex-Crosby, Henry Brogden and Seth Warriner did a fabulous job and the stories are stronger due to their critical input.

I was delighted when Sandra Mangan agreed to be involved with this new set of Tales. Sandra has played an important part in all my writing projects. Yet again, she did a great job during the editing stage.

Big thanks must also go to Val Hall, Christine Seddon and Kendra Allen for taking the time to read through the proof copies before the new Tales were released into the wild.

A Note From The Author

Thank you, reader, for deciding to read the Tales. I have everything crossed that you enjoyed the stories as much as I enjoyed writing them. It's been a while since I wrote the previous set of Tales and it proved quite a challenge to create eight brand-new short stories that felt fresh, entertaining and different. Hopefully, I've achieved what I set out to do.

You could try to create your own Impossible Tale now that you've read mine. Begin with an object or a scenario from real-life then think carefully what could happen. Twist and stretch your ideas; the wackier and weirder they turn out, the better. Let your imagination run wild! Good luck and happy writing.

I love to read. It's one of my favourite things in the world. Books feed my imagination, exercise my brain and help me become a better writer. I always encourage the children I meet to find a book and get reading. There are so many amazing characters, incredible places and wonderful adventures hidden between the covers of books. Dive in and enjoy!

Website: www.danworsley.com
Twitter: @dan__worsley

Printed in Great Britain
by Amazon